TH

2 | THE COMING

By Tyler G. Johnson

4 | THE COMING

What you are about to read is the memory I have of what happened. That calamitous era at the closing of humanity's timeline is over and done, but He found it fitting to have me write its recounting in first person, just as I experienced it.

I am writing from this realm and season to yours. In order to comprehend that concept, you have to understand that when you come here time has no hold on you. We can access any period and look upon it like it is the now. I watched those days and recorded them, for He told me that many of you would need the following pages because of the overwhelming misunderstanding that is pervasive in the minds of religious men in your day. You need to know, once again, to have courage and not to fear, for there truly is no reason to fear.

Some details may be askew, and your upcoming experience may vary from my own in those days, but the general themes need to be taken to heart. If you are to become everything you are destined to be, you must start to look upon the future through the eyes of victory rather than defeat. Either it really was finished when He said it was, or you have a looming battle before you that you cannot win. You must make your choice. His hope is that this book will help you make that choice. The following chapters are not a gloomy warning (you have had enough of that), but a hopeful encouragement to all that have ever looked upon the last days with a defeatist mentality, whether you call it that or not.

I can assure you of three things. First, you will not be whisked away from the trouble, but filled until you overcome it. Second, you will be exceedingly victorious, despite the darkness being poured out. Third, His nature will continue to be most accurately summed up by the word, "Love". Never stray from these realities and you will not only survive the coming days, but prosper.

Your servant, friend, and brother,
Scythe

One

The Seers told us that they couldn't see much further into the future, as though the timeline of mankind ended like a coastal road that suddenly turns into the sea. They informed us that as abruptly as the dropping of the veil at the end of a Shakespeare play, the not-too-distant future became inaccessible by sight. It was the end, or at least near it. This did not upset us.

Though it was unclear what the exact date was, most of us knew that it had been thousands of years since The Bleeding Teacher had walked the earth. I say "most" because time wasn't something the majority of people kept track of anymore. Since calendars had been among the many things destroyed, we simply knew it was day when the sun shone, and night when the moon relieved the sun from its watch. Many felt that was all we needed to know, though there were rumors that there had been periods when even those methods of keeping in step with time had proved unstable and unreliable. Rather than charting our days on calendars as they did in ages past, we spent most of our energy focused on reflecting on what The Eternal was doing or had done rather than remembering what defeats we had weathered. When we did this, we overcame the atrocities that surrounded us.

And that, in short, described us quite accurately; we were triumphant despite the climate of darkness and violence around us. Sometimes even *because* of it. I say that because it was as though in direct relation to an increase of darkness that was poured forth, a greater increase of light and glory was also released as well. We never felt like we didn't have the upper hand, even if it came at the last moment, like hitting an ace on the river.

And that brings me to explain how we viewed our deliverance; it was something that we understood would first and foremost occur on the crust of this planet, not by being taken away from it. We didn't look forward to the end like some form of salvation swooping in to save us. I guess when one tastes of a victorious lifestyle, going back and eating of how they used to live (of fear and cowering and hiding away, hoping to be rescued because one never learned their true identity and authority in the first place), becomes more like digesting poison than just eating old food. It isn't that we would have fought against being taken away, but that we understood that our job was to manifest the realm of Eternal *here* rather than plainly go there. With this understanding in place we were not powerless, knowing that the Answer came from within us rather than from above us. We spent our time transforming the earth rather than promoting the end of it, and the result was that we were not so anxious to leave it as those in past generations.

Today was another gathering. It had been a hard month, with many attacks and losses from The Unenlightened. Many of the The Chosen had been killed, many taken, many brutalized. Even so, we were not deterred in our focus, for it had been foretold that these things would happen. These assailments had caused numerous to relent and give themselves to serve The Unenlightened, but many had also been converted that once served their masses. It seems that travail revealed the true insides of every man and woman like sandpaper reveals the beauty, or rot, of the wood hidden beneath the layers.

As always, our meeting place was kept as unpublicized as possible, with hopes that we could continue for hours without interruption, caught up in the brilliance that we continually experienced. Children would take the stage and speak words of inexpressible encouragement and revelation that men of past centuries had never even thought upon. It came faster than anyone could record by pen. Regularly and without preparation, a song of affection would rise from the voices of thousands, starting and ending at the exact same second, octave, and note. It was as though The Eternal Himself wrote a script for us to follow in our times together that none of us had read. Many times complete silence would take us over; every one of us caught up into heavenly places, interacting with each other not on earth, but elsewhere, far away, for years at a time though it was only hours on earth. In that place were could communicate with extreme clarity, interact with those that had gone on before us, and receive strength for what lay ahead.

Once, during a gathering that had lasted for a few days, in one of these moments of sovereign silence, I came back to this place prematurely. I say "prematurely" because though it had been nearly a decade in the time above, nobody in the mass gathered had arrived back to this realm yet. I came to myself in the midst of the tens of thousands around me, finding the picture comical. They stood around me, every one wide-eyed and jaws extended. The gaping was laughable, which I did as I walked through the crowd. No matter how loud I laughed, none awoke. I would shake some to make sure they still possessed life, for their heartbeat had ceased, but they would never awake. So is the way of love;

nothing can shake you out of this trace of ecstasy, nothing can make you leave until you have had your fill. I later learned that none were ever harmed by these odd experiences that would come over each person in our gatherings. Physical healings happened every time we were together, always restoring those that had been beat and tortured by The Unenlightened, hence why nobody feared their attempted intimidation. Yet now, all manner of diseases and abnormalities were rarely healed at these gatherings, for all had been healed long before, when we started experiencing this new level of power that was being poured out from Above.

It was not just the learned and wise that walked in this unprecedented power, but every person; young to old, stately to lowly, fool to astute. Children on the day of birth, in the greatest state of weakness that any human ever resides within, were regularly laid in the arms of the sick and dying that were unable to make it to our gatherings. Nobody worried that the children would be infected or sickened like we had in the past. We now knew more about the power that the infants and children possessed in their innocence and receptivity. They were born into the Kingdom while it was as though the rest of us were trying to find our way back, like we had all started there only to find ourselves far from home when we had grown up and matured. We spend our lives making our way back to the place where we started.

But it was not just the children that demonstrated their citizenship of another Land. Those well advanced in years also revealed this, yet in another way that was equally impressive. Many in our company claimed to have learned secrets put forth in the writings of old that taught one to believe for longer lifespans. I never had much of a grasp on it, but they swore it was possible if one simply accepted its impossibility in their mind and heart. They said that once they had adjusted their thinking, they simply leaned into those written words of old until one lost their balance and sank into them. They said once they got ahold of you, you couldn't get out. I wasn't sure how that made me feel. When I would tell them that, they insisted that one wouldn't want to be free from them anyways, and that I was missing the whole point. After long enough there they said you would became one with the words. The result was agelessness. A few even claimed to be a few generations old. And we didn't challenge the genuineness of their claims, for many of them seemed to have acute information about events that took place long ago, events that most of us had only heard about from those in our families that had long since gone on. All in all it made me very curious, maybe even uncomfortable, especially when they would talk about the fountain of life that they had discovered and yet would never lead us to geographically.

Whether young or old, grace was over all in different manners and forms, and to such an extent that miracles were more a lifestyle than an event.

It was rumored that the gathering would be in a certain evergreen forest that I was familiar with. Fields had been our choice of meeting place until helicopters started being used to find us. We weren't hard to spot from the air, or hear from miles away. Thus, we now met miles from towns, under the cover of the green branches of coniferous giants.

I left my house slowly, assuring there wasn't anyone else on the small road I lived on. We had to remember to not leave our houses at the same time; a crowd walking in the same direction was suspicious, not to mention completely obtuse of us. As I got out on the main road that cut through town, I surveyed what used to be; our town looked as it had for years, poor. Since the wars had started against us, most buildings had been maimed or flattened completely. They didn't want us to have any kind of economy, let alone places to get goods, such as food.

It always gave me an odd joy to behold this material destruction. Though all of us would still enjoy the material happiness that we once had, the void it left was filled by an increase of focus on a much greater Addiction. But what made me chuckle was that despite The Unenlightened's best efforts to strip us of every necessity to sustain life, we continued to thrive. It was their greatest thorn in the side, proof that The Eternal still existed, was still active, and still on our side. Our mere *existence* was like spit in their faces.

The dirt road made its way out of town and up a long hill that would soon dip and turn for miles. I had almost forgotten where the road led, for it had been long since I had traveled its length. On both sides of the lane the thick forest grew, reaching out to me from the sides of the road with branches, ferns, and other green foliage. I loved my long walks to our outdoor meetings. The Designer was in the green, in the drips that were caught, trapped and held high by the leaves and bryophytes before they were drank by the ground. He was in the light and wind that kissed my face with delicateness and repetition. The maker can be found in what is made.

Though it was quite a distance to my destination, all I needed to do was walk down this road until someone called for me from the depths of the forest. For gatherings like this, the Chosen would set watchmen by the road to signal us into the woods when we were remotely near the meeting place, otherwise we would never find the exact location. Forming something like a long chain made of people, with many hundreds of yards between each link, the watchmen would lead us to the specific location of the meeting place.

After some time of walking past miles of unchanged road and surroundings, I heard someone call to me from the forest. His call was like smoke on the breeze; light, but recognizable.

"Who has chosen you?" he whispered from afar, quietly.

"He has", I replied in a normal tone, knowing that nobody was following me.

Unsatisfied with my answer, my unseen guide, heavily camouflaged and deep in the thick brush said, "Who is He that has chosen you?"

"The One That Bled."

"Come" he said, pointing in a direction away from the road.

This ritual, though not foolproof, was our way of interrogation. It weeded out some of those that were half-hearted in dedication to our gatherings. If the person could not declare allegiance to Him with their mouth, they were not given the direction to the next watchman. Each watchman would address the person walking on the road or through the woods the same way, unflinchingly, firmly, and with the intensity that comes with protecting thousands of lives. Like silent assassins crouched in the shadows, they were not to be trifled with nor taken lightly, but with utmost seriousness. I had heard stories of some of these men not believing the road walkers, and instead of fleeing into the darkness, which would make following them impossible (the established protocol), they further "interrogated" the wanderers. The Seers do not condone or excuse this behavior, but acknowledge that it is understandable, considering the circumstances.

It was safe to assume that the watchman was pointing me in the direction of the next human marker for me to head towards, deep in the woods, possibly but not likely, miles away. Too many got lost (sadly, some never found) in the dense woods when the watchmen spaced themselves out further than a quarter of a mile, and the shouting that some of the Chosen did when they realized they had lost their course just wouldn't do. The watchmen found that more distance could prove to be more dangerous rather than less, so they rarely agreed anymore to put such distance between themselves. If the chain were found, the end of the chain could be found as well, where our unlawful adoration would be abruptly stopped at best, if not completely decimated.

As I left the first watchmen and headed towards the next, I thought upon the times in the past when our meetings had been discovered.

Yes, horrifically, I had been at more than one meeting that had been discovered and broken up. Some of my friends joking called me "The Survivor", but only after I was thoroughly questioned and cleared by the higher authorities in our religious community. Suspicion ran high in my case that I was an informant because I had been in so many of these meetings that were discovered. Of course I was not an informant, but it was only because of my history of extreme dedication, sense of duty to our ideals, and my complete compliance to my spiritual authorities that they believed me. If they hadn't, excommunication was guaranteed; they had to protect the rest of the flock that they watched over.

Not many can speak of making it out of more than one of those types of situations, but I had three times. Once I hid under the body of a woman that had been sprayed by bullets along with everyone else at the gathering. I had rehearsed this type of scenario in my head beforehand, sadly, and was prepared because of it. I simply fell as she fell, appearing as though I had been struck by the bullets as well, though I had not. Once we were down and they weren't looking, I pulled her body up over me so that her body, and the others around me, completely covered me. I was deeply concerned that they would go through the horizontal crowd and put extra bullets in the bodies as they always did, but because of the great numbers that had been at that meeting they ran out of ammunition. The moment they left, many sprang back to life, speaking of residue that was left over from our songs. We gathered again, and continued as we had before our enemies came.

There was another time they found us and the events played out very differently. As always, the people kept singing, determined that nothing would interrupt their melody of love to their Lover. The Unenlightened took their time, loading their guns, laughing, mocking, casually talking to one another about which person they had marked in front of them to shoot, and finally, cocking their guns. If you have ever witnessed the relaxed state a farmer has when he is about to process his pigs or cows, you know what they looked like. Totally unconcerned for the well being of those in front of them, it would not be too much to say that they seemed subtly *excited* about what they were about to do.

With their weapons now ready to shoot, just as they were about to release much lead into the air, a nearby cedar suddenly broke at its base, as if some unseen forced pushed it over with vast strength. If you ask those that were there, most would say it was likely the Winds that did this. The tree, about ten feet wide at the base, broke as simply as a piece of straw does as when a child runs through a field that is dry and ready for harvest. The tree landed on one of their military vehicles, which exploded, and sent all of them into a flurry of fear, running for their lives. Most of those singing didn't even notice, still carrying melody and loudly interceding. More times than I could count on my hand, I had personally witnessed the Winds protect The Chosen, but rarely with my naked eye did I actually *see* them.

That is one reason we had the name we had. Every time we mentioned our name, we were reminded of the *untouchableness* that was about us. We were the Chosen; He was on our side. He was for us; which deductively means that He wasn't for our enemies. Thus, who could be against us?

I found the next "link" in the chain, and he pointed me to the next. This went on a few more times until I came within earshot of the group that had already amassed. Only a few more hundred yards and I would be in their midst, among friends that I had never met, strangers that I could trust fully, and family that was born not of blood, but of spirit. I was nearing, in many ways, home.

Two

The brush was very thick ahead, creating a natural wall-like barrier. As I got closer to the gathering, I could feel something come over my body. My legs grew slightly weak, not in a unpleasant way, but in the way one feels after one has kissed their future spouse for the first time. The air around me seemed to rapidly increase in temperature; it felt the same way a burning wood stove warms your skin when you stand a few feet from it after coming in from the cold. They varied in type, but these were a few of the manifestations I would feel every time I approached one of our gatherings. They brought me peace, for their non-existence meant that it could be a mock meeting, intended to lure The Chosen to a meeting so that all would be arrested.

I had made it to the barrier of brush, and forced my way through it. The woods had been dark, and once I stepped to the other side I was immediately blinded. Light, coming from no place in particular, was shining and illuminating the meeting place. People were singing, some were dancing, some facedown on the dirt and quiet. Others still were very loud, and if it weren't for the atmosphere of that place, it probably would have been very irritating to me.

Something about that place translated everything that came out from every person's mouth into beauty and freedom. It was the oddest thing, but someone with an incredibly gifted voice was just as pleasant to listen to as the chap that was screaming. It was clear that he wasn't screaming in pain or sadness, but yelling nonetheless. The most peculiar part was that every time he let loose an undignified scream, the weakness in my legs and the heat that encompassed me would increase. It was though the essence of freedom was being released as he let loose such a coarse sound. I stayed near this man for a while, drinking from that which he was pouring out.

I wondered if there was anyone there that I would recognize, so I moved on, and tried to make my way towards the general center of this sea of humanity.

Not long after that, I noticed a friend that I had met at a gathering a few months back. She, like many, never left the meetings, going from one to another. My story was different. I felt that my time in the town, with The Unenlightened, though risky, was needed. I reasoned that there was no other way they would convert if we weren't in their midst.

Rachel was turned away from me now, so I walked up behind her and hugged her from behind, startling her. She spun around, smiled as she saw that it was me, and hugged me back.

"Scythe! It is good to see you." She said eagerly. "Have you heard what the Seers are saying we need to do tonight?" She asked.

"No, I just arrived."

"Many are hungry. The food banks in most towns have been destroyed or pilfered. They are saying that if we repent for our faults and ask for help from on high, we will see people fed tonight."

Call me daft, but it was only then that I noticed; most of the people that were around me were crying out for mercy; emaciated and desperate. Those that were on their face in the dirt were loudly begging for food. My heart broke for these needy ones, and I joined in with their cry. Maybe one more person pushing in prayer would bring the breakthrough they needed.

Nearby, without anyone announcing it, people began throwing scraps of food into the middle of a circle that was opening up in the crowd. Half eaten corn on the cob, a small potato, a dried piece of cheese; these were the sacrifices that others made hoping to contribute to the widespread need for sustenance. The scraps became a small pile, barely enough to feed even a small boy, pathetic to look at, but for many it was salvation in the dirt.

I was well fed. Somehow I always managed to come across food, always in ridiculously wonderful ways. Once I was walking alongside a lake on my way to another meeting, praying about the fact that I wanted to *choose* to go on fasts rather than forced into it due to my circumstances. The moment that thought left my heart, a full-grown Sockeye salmon jumped out of the water and landed on the sand in front of me. It was deep red, ready to spawn, and had made its way up the river that led into the lake I was walking by. I picked it up and ate well for a few days. Stories of provision like this happened regularly to all, though there were times when we gathered to ask as a corporate body for provision when it was lacking.

The pile of scraps was suddenly growing, getting taller and wider, visually noticeable to all. Some began to cheer, and parents released the hands of hungry children so that they could storm the base of the pile in joy. Now taller than anyone present, the pile had grown with extreme speed, but one couldn't really put their finger on how exactly. The science of how it was happening escaped me, shadowed by the greater reality that it had in fact happened.

There was now food enough for everyone. No longer was the pile one of scraps, but whole foods; full pieces of corn, with each kernel being the size of a small grape, bursting with flavor and warm juice. The hard morsel of cheese had become not a wedge, but the entire circular piece, the kind that is cured in a damp basement in France and requires muscle to pick up. Red, white, and sweet potatoes rolled down the walls of the pile, caught by some that were ready to cook them in a nearby fire.

The nature of the gathering now changed from intensity to joy and gladness. It looked more like a party than anything else. Some still sung and prayed, but most talked with one another as they ate their otherworldly-birthed food, laughing and enjoying each other's company.

Rachel made her way over me with a smug look on her face. "Told you so" she said with a grin.

"I believed you!" I said as I laughed. "It has happened too many times for me to not believe it will happen. It would take more faith to believe it won't happen than it does to believe it will!" We both chuckled, and at that moment I felt my spirit weave itself with Rachel's, delighting in her as The Eternal does. This was where we found true fellowship; a place where connection wasn't dependent upon gender, race, or denomination.

I surveyed those that were there, numbering around 3,000. Again, it struck me; the vast gamet of differing denominational backgrounds that we all had prior to the present years of power. Those that used to be of various beliefs and denominations (ones that were diametrically opposed to one another) now all melded together as one. Many had even forgotten what denomination they used to ascribe to; it was that inconsequential now. During these days what joined us together was no longer our agreement of theological disposition or denomination, but spiritual fathers. We rallied around fathers that we could follow rather than doctrines that we could not. We had outgrown our previous ways, accepting each other, attempting to function in honor at all times. And over the years, we had seen our worldwide community transform from divisiveness and arguing, only being able to agree on a few basic truths, into a group of people that acted like royalty towards each other. We have a saying, "Every one is a king and queen, to the youngest of age." Every time two people would interact, it was as though both were talking to the King of Britain. Thus, we found that if we lived by honor first and foremost, and had leaders that modeled it as well, theological differences were put on the shelf. We even began to *value* each other's theological differences, for in some cases one's perspective was more effective than the other, when at other times it was the other way around.

Rachel and I sat down, caught up, and ate a small meal. Time was different when all of us were together; it went fast, validating the saying, "Time flies when you are having fun."

Before long, the sun was setting, and my long walk back into the town would prove to be near to impossible if I didn't start off soon. I said goodbye to Rachel, kissed her cheek, and made my way out of the gathering. Affection like I had shown to Rachel was not uncommon, even between men and women, and not misunderstood. Love was no longer misunderstood for lust or perversion, and did not lure one's heart into the open to be wounded. Our times above, when our communication lacked the fog that plagues the minds when on earth, always kept us in a place of understanding one another's hearts and intentions.

The long walk through the woods was unaided by the watchmen, for they knew that the dirt road ran somewhat straight and I would unavoidably run across it at some point. I plotted a course into the woods and started on my way, through the woods, down the road, into town, and towards my house.

A few blocks away from my home, I circled around behind the line of houses that included my own, scaled my neighbor's fence, and quietly walked through his dimly lit yard in the light of the moon. Once across the yard, I climbed up a partial wall, reached up and grasped the top of the fence that bordered my own yard, lifted myself up, and peered over. All looked calm, with no visitors.

I would routinely enter my own house in this manner. Coming through the back deterred peering eyes from within the neighborhood, or anyone stationed outside my house, ordered to watch me. Coming home after sunset night after night does not work to your advantage when trying to build a case against the belief that you are spending your nights in prayer with thousands of other people. It didn't look like I wouldn't have to feed them one of typical, half-truth excuses; "I was out foraging for food" or "I was attending to the sick", or my personal favorite, "Visiting the dead." I would smile on the inside, even laugh, when I told them these things, but my exterior would show the greatest amount of sorrow I could muster up. They, on the other hand, *would* smile, even laugh, especially to the "visiting the dead" excuse. Our demise gave them joy. But little did they know, when our "visiting" was over, those that we came to see were as alive as ever.

With that brief gust of wind that rushes past your face when you fall from menial heights, I jumped from my perch on top of the fence, and landed as quietly as I could on the other side. Still cautious, I opened the back door slowly, looking inside as I did.

The door opened to a hallway that had doors on both sides, ending in the living room. If I looked carefully from where I was standing in the frame of the backdoor, I could see all the way through the house and out the front windows of the living room. I squinted my eyes, trying to see if there was a car parked in front of my house; an obvious warning to me that someone had been sent on a stake out.

As I peered I noticed that here was no car but something much worse; not outside, but within the walls of my house. As I let my eyes slowly travel from the floor of my living room and up, searching through the darkness and adjusting from the moonlight outside, I started to make out some sort of foreign form, its reality slowly taking shape in my mind.

It was the outline of a man hidden in the shadows, uninvited, unwelcomed, and standing in the corner of my living room.

24 | THE COMING

Three

"I can see you, you know. What are you doing here?" I blurted out in a flash of both boldness and fear, ripping apart the silence all around me.

"You have very little room to talk to me like that, Scythe. Mind your tongue" the figure replied.

"What are you doing here?" I insisted.

"You know why I am here. We know all about you. We know you are a survivor as well. And we know what you were doing tonight."

"I went for a walk. Is that illegal now too?" I said sarcastically.

In one instant he had crossed the entire distance of the house, from the far corner of the living room to the back door where I stood, and was now close enough that I could feel, and smell, the rot on his breath. "Don't treat me as a blithering idiot, you foul swine. I could end you in the blink of an eye." His nose turned up one corner in disgust. "We know you were not simply *walking* tonight, and even if you were, your thoughts were likely joined Above because of it anyways! Either way you are guilty and will be condemned."

"I don't have time for this. I need sleep. Do whatever you want to do to me, but you and I both know that you have no proof of anything you want to convict me of."

"The time is coming when we will not need proof, only suspicion" He replied with repugnance.

He was right. The Unenlightened, though now quickly deteriorating morally, had started with many checks and balances, accountabilities, and even strived for justice. Mind you, what *they* called justice. Sadly, the implications of that word hinges upon the definition of what is right and wrong by the one wielding it. Thus, just about everyone seems to have a different idea of what it looks like. Hitler thought it would be an injustice to the Arian race to not destroy the Jews. He was convinced they were poisoning humanity's universal pool of DNA and genetic makeup, thus, *his* justice involved killing innocent people.

While they started with general restrictions on what they could and couldn't do, over the years The Unenlighted were cleared to work in many ways that did not follow traditional protocol. Search warrants were now seen as a myth of old; nobody could imagine the humane conduct that would be synonymous with such a law.

The Unenlightened included virtually everyone apart from The Chosen; it was not too extreme a statement to say that the whole world was literally against us, for it was true. They consisted people from all walks of life; all levels of government, housewives, artists, teachers, you name it. The man standing inches from my face was one of them, not too far lost to be converted, but the likelihood was always slim unless they witnessed something extraordinary. I decided to put a proverbial bullet in the conversational gun that was already aimed at my head, drastically changing the direction of our dialogue, and said "You know He is real. I believe you know that He cares for you as well. Believe tonight and leave your allegiance."

And for a moment, almost too quick to notice, I saw the rigidity wane, replaced with a subtle expression of slight inquisitiveness, then washed away by anger, too strong to be genuine; probably a front.

"Who is *He* you refer to? I assure you I haven't the slightest idea. The Enlightened is my redemption, my religion, my life. I will never leave." He started out strong, but I thought I heard his voice start to crack towards the end of his sentence but like a bamboo stick used one to many times for a pole-vault event. He turned away, muttered bitterly about me to himself, as though he was convincing himself afresh of what he had just said. Then, without warning, he stormed out the front door, slamming it so hard that it shook the house, and a picture of me in uniform fell to the floor and shattered.

That picture had been hanging in the hallway for years, taken when I was just as blind as him, serving the same forces as he was, and killed as many, or more, as I suspect he had.

I got into bed, pulled the covers up over my fatigued body, and fell fast asleep.

28 | THE COMING

Four

The light broke through the blinds on my window as invasively as the man had to my house the night before. I was still tired, not ready to awake, but it was rumored that the walk to today's gathering was long, and I needed to get started early in the day if I were to make it.

I got up, dressed, drank some water I had saved from the last spring that the earth had given up at my command, and headed out the front door. That was probably my first mistake, but I wasn't thinking about how to play it safe today. Instead, I was trying to think of what would possess that man, the Unenlightened one, to come into my house at night when I was away. Was he looking for evidence against me, such as the holy writings of old? If so, why wasn't my house torn apart from the search? Was he on a stakeout and decided to saunter inside for a bit? I couldn't piece together what would cause him to come inside, then leave with such haste, without harming me or taking me in to the authorities. Something was awry, but in the midst of this confusion there was an unavoidable peace that would not leave my heart despite its concerns.

My walk was enjoyable as usual, and I eventually made my way to the exact meeting location the Seers had determined. Many were there, flooding the forest with movement and life. A stage of sorts had been constructed by the laying of downed trees together side-by-side, then more layers stacked on top. It looked primitive, nonetheless quite an accomplished feat considering that it was done without the help of machinery.

The Seers came onto the stage, followed by a laughing and dancing mass of children. With a bright smile, one of the Seers raised his voice to address the crowd of people before him, stretching into the woods as far as he could see.

"Celebration for what He has done for us is our priority today." Though he spoke without amplification of a microphone and speakers, his voice carried throughout the entire crowd with ease, as though the Winds carried his words to each individual's ears. "Let us give Him the honor He deserves!"

With that, joy broke out, and explosively so. People started jumping as though they were standing on hot coals, not being able to stay still. The ground began to shake with a peculiar pattern. After a few seconds I realized that the jumping was in such exact synchronization that it was creating a defined beat, with no instruments except the feet of those dancing hitting the earthen floor. Singing and shouting was added to this organic composition, creating a forestral orchestra.

Our song continued for quite some time, all thoroughly enjoying themselves. An odd satisfaction would well up inside your being at times like this; a feeling that every need you had was being fully met. We were totally satisfied. Each and every one of us could honestly say that there was nowhere else we would want to be, as though heaven had actually come down and made Its abode on the earth. We didn't beg for The Eternal to come, we delighted in the fact that He was there, fully meeting our every desire by simply being *near*.

Then slowly, the beat held by our dance upon the ground began to shift. I noticed that it wasn't that the rhythm was changing to another tempo, but that it was being lost altogether. Something else was making the earth shake. As our song decreased, this new sound increased and took its place. It was a unsettling rumbling; the sound modernity, of metal, and man.

Suddenly the sound came into view. Tearing towards our dancing company was a large row of off road vehicles, even a tank. I thought their aggressive intrusion was ridiculously laughable; as though we were any sort of threat to them to begin with. They came barreling into the woods, swerving through the trees and breaking down the brush, as though they were pushing forward on the frontlines of battle. The crowd calmly parted as the procession of vehicles parked side by side in front of the stage, forming a long line. Dust and dirt were riled into the air, causing those nearby to cough and choke.

Out of each vehicle came one or more of the Unenlightened. Their every movement emitted arrogance and hate, and an unseen cloud of blackness overshadowed them. One man seemed to be the commanding officer on the scene for he rode in the tank, was the first to speak, and was the only one that did not have a full-faced ski mask pulled over his face. I deducted that at least in part, he did not wear a mask because he felt no shame for what he was about to do.

"What do we have here?" he sneered. "This is very dishonoring to our system of justice. Every country in the world has agreed that this is not lawful, why cannot you?" He waited for a response, as if someone in the crowd would have something to say then continued, "Thus, in order to right the scales of justice today, there must just be punishment. I am merciful and just, therefore only those that are on the stage this day will die."

And with that, each masked soldier crawled up to stand on the top of his vehicle, cocked his gun, and picked his target. Those on the stage froze in disbelief.

There is a very disconcerting moment in life; found after a gun has been readied to shoot, and before it is shot. Nobody breathes, nobody moves. Much like the moment after "SET" has been proclaimed at a track event, everything is wound up tight by a silent anxiety, ready to snap at any instant. Everyone is waiting for the inevitable to happen, hoping that for some reason it may not. But nothing stopped these guns from firing this time. The Winds did not keep the triggers from being pressed, and bullets were fired.

And unexpectedly, everything went into slow motion. It was as though I could see every shot forced out of each fiery barrel. I watched as the ammunition slowly flew through the air and struck each victim, slashing through their frail bodies. Innocent and beautiful, they fell like wilting flowers, every one of them. I had seen death before, but this struck me anew. Sorrow and anger, even hatred, flooded my being. I wanted to kill in return, and I would have if it had had a weapon. This was wrong.

But the cruelty that most stole my attention was a child near the edge of the stage, not more than four feet away and above of me. Blonde hair, no more than 5 years old, had been shot three times across the chest.

Death is such a gruesome, unjust thing. It comes without mercy and steals that which we most love.

This little boy stumbled back and forth on the stage, fighting against the lead that had fatally wounded his body. I didn't doubt that somewhere nearby in the crowd was the mother of this child, fully witnessing her son's death. He lurched to the edge of the stage, misplaced his last steps, and began to fall.

I moved like lighting towards his falling body and managed to catch him before he pounded the earth. Those around me blurred and took on an odd sense of insignificance as all of my focus narrowed in on this little one.

I looked him in the face as I held him in my arms. He was gasping for air, with a terrified look of surprise and fear on his face. Now surveying his body, I saw that the three shots had punctured his lungs, explaining the short, exasperated breaths of air that he was fighting for. His body lurched back and forth with each breath, and soon he wouldn't have the energy to fight for oxygen anymore.

Many thoughts come to you in situations like this, but most of all you are aware that you don't know what to do. In a desperate attempt to do something to help, I laid him down on the ground and applied pressure to the holes in his chest that were spilling out precious blood. I pressed my hands over those holes, hoping that maybe I could keep some of this liquid of life inside his body while someone else mended this child with a tourniquet fashioned out of a portion of their shirt. Better yet, I hoped that as I kept pressure on his chest someone would go to the town to find medical supplies. But neither of these scenarios was applicable this day. We were too far from town to get there and back in time, plus there were no supplies for us to use in the old medical facility. And no tourniquet would stop this torrent of blood pouring from his chest.

All I could do was hold pressure on two of the three holes at a time with my hands, changing their position when the uncovered hole would again start to bleed badly. If I had another hand, I would have used it.

Then it happened. I moved one of my hands from one of the bullet holes to another, and lost sight of the one I had just been holding. I ripped open the child's shirt and brought my face down towards his skin, looking closely in disbelief. Either the hole wasn't there anymore or I was starting to see things. Now there seemed to be only two holes. I reassured myself that there were only two holes all along, resisting the tempting thought that I was going mad.

The boy's breathing started to calm and I assumed that his body was giving out on him, too tired to fight anymore. "At some point death comes for us all" I thought to myself, trying to bring my heart some kind of numbing solution for the moment.

Then, his eyes opened with a brightness that every five-year-old wears, and he smiled at me. I thought to myself, "He must have been he was having an experience associated with the fact that he was near death; maybe the cliché tunnel of light or heavenly voices." We had seen this before in massacre situations. It seems whether the will of the Eternal is completely fulfilled or not, He and His workers would still show up just to receive the one in death, and while receiving, giving peace to all around.

I looked up towards the crowd, hoping to spot his mother. I figured it was her last chance to say goodbye to her little boy, and he needed the comfort she would bring. Suddenly, he reached up and pulled my hands off his chest as he giggled, "I can't breath when you press so hard!"

I took away my hands in surprise, first that he was smiling, then that he was struggling to his feet. I pulled back his torn shirt draping over his chest to find soft, unbroken skin underneath. Standing, he hugged me, then ran into the crowd, where his weeping mother met him. There was so much turmoil going on with the chaos of vehicles leaving, dust swirling in the air, and people praying loudly, that I don't think many had witnessed what had just happened. I confess I began crying, motivated by relief, but more so, thankfulness and awe.

My tears caught me off guard. We had seen The Eternal intervene before, for He was always moving on our behalf. We were used to the miraculous. But there were times like this were something happened in a new and glorious way that ambushed me with a fresh understanding of The Eternal's abilities.

Regardless if we realize it or not, we all have things we believe are impossible until we witness The Eternal break the impossibility like straw. Our understanding shifts, but we are impressed once again when He does a new thing that we never dreamed was possible. Perhaps this is one of our greater weaknesses as human beings, or perhaps it is simply the result of living in a natural world with limitations and physical laws that we are forced to become accustomed to. Ironically, we spend the first few years of our lives learning of these physical laws and limitations, only to spend the rest of our lives attempting to unlearning them. We call that faith.

And though I had seen death before, emotion was nonetheless drowning me. There were both good and bad emotions sweeping over me, for I was still recovering from both the horror and joy that had taken place moments before. It was only then that I was able to admit to myself that the boy's breathing had calmed minutes before because he was being made well, not because he was nearing death, and that the third bullet hole *had* in fact vanished, followed by the other two as well.

Then out of nowhere, something hard struck my head with incredible force, dizzying me. Suddenly I found myself being drug backwards across the ground by my collar, choking me of air. I was lifted up and thrown, landing on a seat inside one of the vehicles. For a brief second my face, now dripping with blood, was pressed against the cool of a black leather seat, then juggled away as I was tossed about in the moving vehicle. We were speeding over the makeshift path in the woods that the Unenlightened's vehicles had plowed only minutes before.

I was starting to recuperate from the reeling of my head; the inside of the truck was starting to cease from spinning. My captor still wore his mask, and didn't say anything until we had reached the dirt road.

"I saw what happened back there," He said sternly.

"I'm sorry?" I fired back, enraged. "Are you referring to the fact that you and your "army of liberation" just gunned down innocent people, or the fact that you just pistol whipped me in the side of the head and kidnapped me?"

"And I must apologize for the hit to the head. I had to make it look convincing to those watching…"

"You succeeded! What did you accomplish by hitting me?"

He ignored my question and picked up from where he had left off. "…But I did not kill anyone today, though my colleagues did. I hope there is forgiveness for such carnage, for in the end, it is my fault."

Forgiveness? Was this man schizophrenic? Why did he care in the least bit about forgiveness? Question after question rushed through my mind. But instead of tending to my questions first, the blood that was wetting the right side of my head took precedence.

"Do you have a rag that I can use to wipe up this blood?" He reached into the backseat and handed me a towel, then a first aid kit. His kindness pertaining to my physical condition surprised me; either I was being set up or this man had a secret to tell.

"What do you mean by you didn't kill anyone today. You had a gun, and you shot it."

"Yes, but I aimed high."

"You intentionally missed? Why?" I asked, still enraged. I had not yet calmed from the dreadfulness we were driving away from and was entertaining the idea of revenge, imagining the bloodied towel in my hands as a noose around his neck.

With that, he pulled off his ski mask. I was surprised to see a familiar face underneath. It was the man that had been in my house the night before.

"Because I cannot avoid what is becoming clear to me", He said calmly, with a humility that I couldn't avoid to take note of.

"What is clear to you?" I asked, feeling as though I had to dig into him for each minuscule detail that I needed.

"That my destiny is to serve the same power as you."

38 | THE COMING

Five

I couldn't have been more surprised. When he had first thrown me into the car, I was sure he was going to take me out in the woods and give me one to the back of the skull. Instead, he was confessing to me the most illegal of all crimes; his desire to join the ranks of the Chosen.

"How on earth did you come to that conclusion?" I asked him in disbelief.

"It was a mounting reality. It started with visitations at night and ended today at our 'intervention'. I would go to bed at night to be awaked not long after by a Being of light in my room. Waves of liquid radiance would wash over me, as real as water from a showerhead. He would tell me only one thing each time he came; "I love you". It was a matter of time before I believed him. I knew he was not aligned with the sources of power the Enlightened serve..."

"You mean Unenlightened, correct?" I interrupted with a half smile.

"Yes, pardon me. Unenlightened. I suppose that is something I will have to start to get used to. Anyways, I knew He was not like the powers I am familiar with, for He brought me peace inside, and them, fear. Also, His words were not just words, but had real material worth. When He spoke, I could physically feel his words affect my whole being, changing me. Yet, I still didn't know who He was exactly. Since He wasn't of a power I knew, I entertained He was the source of power that the Chosen, as you call yourselves, followed. Today, when I saw the child restored in your arms, it pushed me over the edge. I knew that the only Being of love that was capable of such an act was the same that has been meeting me in the night season. A name was put to a face. What do you call Him anyways?"

"'Love' will do. Call Him what you may; He answers to many names, for it is not the name that lures Him but the state of heart that calls. This is why many that have never known of Him are visited, and many that are not seeking have been found."

"I see. How is your head now? Better?"

"Yes, thank you. The bleeding has seemed to have stopped. And why were you in my house last night? Were you looking for something?"

"Yes and no. I had been sent to stakeout your house. Once I was sure you were not inside, but at one of your gatherings, I went inside to find anything that would answer my question of who this Man was that visited me at night. He haunted me more than the souls of those I have killed for converting to the Chosen, wonderfully so, but nonetheless haunted. He would not leave me alone. I went inside your house hoping that I could find something that would inform me about Him, but also to talk to you in private, where nobody would see me, and ask you the sensitive questions that I am now. When you came home, you startled me, and I grew defensive out of fear that my curiosities would be discovered. When you told me that He cared for me, it hit too close to home, with me knowing that I couldn't avoid the truth any longer. My world spun, and I left."

I liked him. He spoke simply and directly, with a clear sense of honesty about him. He was real, genuine, and

I could see that his heart had been changed from a dull fragment of steel to a thing of flesh and feeling.

"You said that the massacre today was your fault. Why is that?" I asked

"When you left your house today, I followed you. Once I found the location of the meeting, I went back and reported it to my supervisors. I didn't think that they would kill anyone, but simply break it up with force." His voice began to fracture, and huge tears of sorrow and regret began to well up in his eyes, falling to his lap. "Children were there. And nobody was even taking of the bread and wine, where the power is released that we fear! They were just dancing!"

He was practically howling in regret now, very undignified for the Unenlightened, and I could feel the reality of guilt, shame, and regret actually pressing down on him in the truck. He needed to taste of the grace I had become so accustomed to, covering over my imperfections and making me perfect, day after day.

"It is time my friend." I said gently. And with a mounting sense of authority, I declared to him, "You are forgiven. May the blood of the Undying be upon you. Guilt, shame, and condemnation be removed. Freedom, you who possesses the heart that knows it is delighted in, come *now*! Come kiss his soul!"

The moment those words came out of my mouth he slumped over in the driver's seat, like he had taken a blow to head akin to my own. That subtly pleased me. The horn responded, as it should when something hits the center of the steering wheel, and the truck began to lose control. I quickly pulled my unconscious friend out of the drivers seat and began to drive.

I hadn't driven in years, and it felt good. The horn must have been heard by other vehicles, because some pulled over alongside the road to wait for me, while others sped up behind me. They must have interpreted the horn to mean that my driver, still nameless to me, was alerting them of some problem. Thankfully, the tinted windows kept them from seeing who the actual driver was now, but nonetheless, I had to lose them until my friend awoke from his blacking out.

So I gunned it. When I say "gunned" it, I mean that I was already going about 45 miles per hour on this dirt road, and when I accelerated, the rear tires lost grip and spun, which I liked. I had always liked speed. I quickly gained enough momentum to create quite a cloud of dust behind me, for it hadn't rained for a few days and the road was dry, making enough of a blinding mess that it made it hard for anyone to follow very close behind me. I slid corners and flew on straight a ways. I knew that while the dust had been my rescuer for the time being, soon it would work to my disadvantage, showing exactly where I had been, making me easy to track. The helicopters would be out soon, so I needed to get far away as quickly as possible, so I took the first paved road that I found, and the cloud behind me vanished.

My friend was now waking, but still not completely his restrained self. It was as though someone had forced him to drink a large amount of alcohol, for he was slurred in speech, and not making any sense when he did manage to form coherent words. His laughter was the disconcerting sort that you hear in mental hospitals, unrestrained and long, though not lack it at all in that it didn't lack true happiness. It made me glad and uncomfortable at the same time. I decided that until this oddity wore off, I would continue to drive.

I had seen this condition before. Some called it "The Sign of Immersion", or "The Drowning Miracle", both too vague and mysterious for me. I simply believe it was when Love came and took your breath, only to replace it with Itself. One would sometimes black out in the most desirable way, like the fainting a woman does when kissed by the man of her dreams. It is a moment that feels as if every dream has come true. You feel completely powerful, full of love, and most of all, raw, uncontrollable, unmaintained joy. My captor was in the thick of it, and if there was one thing I had learned from my own experience was that the greatest injustice another could do to him was awaken him from this ecstasy before he was ready to leave it. Therefore, I let him enjoy this new experience and resigned myself to the driver's seat.

Most of the drive was enjoyable, despite the hyena-like cackling beside me, but there were a few moments that worried me.

At one point, off in the distance, I could manage to make out a few cars pulled off to the side of the road. The lights on the top of their car were already on, spinning in the typical blue and reds, communicating to me that I needed to pull over. Someone must have radioed ahead and reported some suspicious activity because of the way I had needed to drive in order to get away from the other vehicles on the dirt road. I could have put my new convert at the wheel, but I didn't think he possessed the needed faculties of coordination and speech, so that was no option. To remedy the situation, I did the very thing you wouldn't think to do when clearly signaled by the authorities to slow down and pull over. I sped up. By the time I passed my stationary rivals, I was going well over 100 mph. Their catching up with me was a distant dream. I flew past them with the window down, smiling and waving, just to spite them.

My inebriated companion eventually came back to his right mind, though he said that he didn't really want to, never having felt such acceptance and freedom.

"Can you hear me, my friend?" I asked the unmasked convert.

"Yes, course of! Excuse me, I mean of course!"

"What is your name?"

"Echelon."

"My name is Scythe. It is nice to meet you properly." I said as a genuine smile stretched across my face.

I assured Echelon that such an experience would happen again, in fact, anytime that he wanted it to. We switched places and he started the long drive back to town, planning to come into town from the opposite direction that we had left from, hoping to keep from being seen by anyone searching for Echelon's truck. As dusk fell, we parked behind an abandoned shack a few blocks from my house, walked home, and went inside. Night was upon us, and both of us were ready to retire to bed.

As Echelon turned into his bedroom, he said, "Thank you my friend. I feel as though I am a new creation."

"You are. You are also now adopted into a lineage of greatness, with family abundant. You are now one of us, received, and loved. Sleep well tonight, for tomorrow is the first full day you will have ever truly lived."

Six

I awoke to the sound of droplets of water colliding with the roof, though precipitation had been rare. It was a spring day, the kind that is clear and bright yet full of scattered rains, an environmental setting that makes for wonderful rainbows. Everything spoke of the redemption that I had witnessed the night before in the truck of The Unenlighted, now truly enlightened.

Echelon and I decided that we would walk to the nearest gathering to let the Seers know what had taken place the day before. We knew that, though slower, walking would attract less attention than Echelon's truck, so we set out on foot for the wooded gathering place.

Understandably, Echelon wasn't exceedingly excited about coming before the Seers, for he was enormously responsible for many of their successor's deaths. He had either directly or indirectly killed their fathers, their friends, their heroes. I assured him that he would find grace before them, and that they had become quite accustomed to forgiving on such an extraordinary level.

The air was pleasantly crisp and clean, making the back of my throat chill slightly when I took in a deep breath. We walked down a narrow path, one used only rarely by those in the town, maybe because of its look. The path was gloriously unmaintained, with the tree branches unkempt and uncut, reaching out over the path above our heads the way a child grabs after something sweet that they want in their parent's hand. The undergrowth and trees made a natural corridor, a tunnel made of a plethora of photosynthetic matter, casting emerald color all around us. It felt safe there, beautiful, and caused one to want to ask questions that you wouldn't normally ask. Questions of depth seemed appropriate here, while a cold, grey, loud room may have stewarded shallow conversation better.

"I have been thinking upon your name lately." I said.

"Yes, what about it? Echelon replied.

"Who gave it to you?"

"My former religion. They gave it to me after I had thoroughly proved my allegiance."

"Ah, I see. Quite a literal name then, isn't it? Feels very mechanical and metal. I'm not sure it fits the state of mind you are in now. You have been brought into a paradigm of grace. Performance is no longer a trait to value, and won't get you promotion like it used to. Now your promotion comes through believing, even if it is in something impossible. The Eternal is pleased only by faith."

"I understand. I will try to do that. I mean, I won't try. Uh, never mind. I understand what you are saying."

I chuckled, as did he. "A change may be in the works. Anything in mind for your new name? I asked.

"No, I hadn't thought about it until now. If it is changed, could we fashion me something that emphasizes grace? I feel that will probably be the theme of my life." He said with a smile.

"Of course. I'm sure the Seers have already become aware of what the Eternal has given you. Most likely, they will let you know when we see them without us ever even mentioning this conversation. They hear much."

"I look forward to it. And what of your name? Is it spelled the way it sounds; like a long exhale one makes when they are a bit frustrated with someone or something?"

That gave me a bit of a laugh. "No. It has little to do with sighing, but with reaping. If you have ever heard of a sickle then you are on the right track "

"Ah yes. Of course. Now I am tracking." Echelon said.

We walked past the first watchman that had sounded to us from the path, and made our way into the forest, stepping over wonderfully decomposed stumps and fallen old-growth trees that had become the foundation and feast, for newer, younger trees.

We neared the meeting and I spotted the Seer that was officiating. One knew who they were by how they dressed, not in an extravagance materially, but in the aura that surrounded them. What exuded from them was as real as any clothing. Maybe Moses veiled his face because it was hard to look at, or maybe it was because he didn't want the people to know when the glory left. We will never know. But *this* glow was nothing short of fantastic, and a joy to behold. Many people would simply stand near the Seers during the songs we sung because the glow had the ability to rub off on those nearby. And when it got on you, it had a vast measure of effects. For one, it almost had a literal taste, though there was nothing in your mouth. The smell was unavoidably magnificent. The Seers told us it was what the Room of Thrones smelled like, and it had gotten on them when they sat there years before. There had been more than one occurrence where The Unenlightened had converted simply because of this aroma.

"Scythe, I am glad to see that you are alive, faithful brother!" the Seer said as he walked up to me and embraced me. His hug was firm and gentle at the same time. "We were worried when we heard that soon after the recent massacre you were taken by one of the Unenlightened in their truck, not to be seen for the rest of yesterday night."

"Yes, I am well. No need to worry."

"Well I know that my son! But who is this? Why is he here?" He said as he took a hesitant step back, looking at Echelon. "You here to steal our loved ones and stop our veneration of The Eternal?"

"No sir. In fact I am here to ask for..."

"Ask for what? Don't you think you have taken enough from us already?" The Seer asserted.

Echelon stumbled to find the right words, "I am sorry sir, pardon me, Seer. I have changed, I mean, been changed."

"Sorry is worthless if the act continues. I need to know that things have changed."

"He has changed, my brother." I said to the Seer. "He has repented, encountered Love Divine, and will not turn back."

"You are sure he is not here to deceive us and find our location? How can you be sure?" The Seer said.

Could I trust him? I hadn't even thought to ask myself this obvious question. I looked into the eyes of my friend that I just met the night before. His eyes spoke of honesty, of hunger for something more. I reasoned that I had no reason not to believe him, for though he had a past marred by sin, ever since I had met him he had acted completely appropriately, never doing anything that caused suspicion to arise in my heart.

"I can be sure because of the peace in my spirit I have when I am with him. He is clean. With all due respect, elder, hear him out. Hear his heart." I said.

"Alright. Speak, you."

"I came to ask you for forgiveness. I am sorry for the life I have lived. I have done many horrible things, things that grieve my heart to think upon." At this point, my friend began to cry again, and I placed my hand on his shoulder as he spoke. "Please" he choked, "Forgive me for what I have done."

"You deserve hell, but yes, I forgive you. Stop crying, you are forgiven." As the Seer said this, he made a cross movement with his hand over Echelon's head.

I was glad to see this forgiveness, though it didn't feel like *grace* per say. No matter, Echelon had been forgiven, and I hoped that the weight that was carried in his heart would be lifted.

"Scythe, you are always used for harvest, aren't you? Always living in such a way so that your name becomes more of a description than a title." The Seer said as he gave me a hearty pat on the back.

"It just happens. I don't know why I am used for this over and over." The Seer, whose exact name I wasn't aware of, was referring to the other Unenlightened that I had led into our company. It happened regularly for me. A person's name can manifest in two ways; to reflect their destiny, or to reflect who they can become without the Eternal. For example, my name can be interpreted two ways; a tool used for harvest, or a bringer of death.

"Well, whatever the reason for why it happens, we are proud of you. In fact, you have been brought up in the Counsel. We have a matter of great urgency for you to attend to. And now that I think of it, your friend, now named Timoria, may be of some help as well."

"We are available for anything the Counsel desires. We would never desire to dishonor our covering through the lack of obedience." I said.

"Good. Follow me." He responded.

"And may I ask, why that name for Echelon?" I asked, curious of the destiny my friend would have.

The Seer simply smiled, turned, and led us away from the gathering, I supposed, towards the locale of the Counsel of The Seers.

Seven

We followed the Seer to a undisclosed location, one that was not publicized to anyone but the Counsel. Even the Chosen were not aware of this place's location, and we had been led into a room without any real knowledge of where we were, for our heads had been covered by a sackcloth bag while we were standing in the woods. We looked as though we had been kidnapped, but the willing cannot be categorized as such. I had a suspicion that we were somewhere underground, because we had made our way down stairs at some point, and the room had the smell of a basement with the familiar feeling of a heightened amount of moisture in the air.

The bags came off our heads and we found ourselves in a large, rectangular room, full of Seers. I had no idea there were so many in existence. Most likely they had been assembled from lands of great distances away. They filled the dimly lit room and were gathered around a circular table, which sat directly in the middle of the cold room. It suddenly occurred to me that this was no standard meeting, and the cause for which they were all brought together must have been of paramount importance.

Echelon, which I assumed was now called Timoria, seemed uncomfortable, fidgeting in the plastic seat he was sitting in.

"How can we be of service, my lords?" I said with the utmost respect and honor.

"We have become aware of a situation. But before we delve into the intricacies of that matter, we will speak to your friend. Timoria, is it, correct?" They turned their attention to my restless friend.

He smiled and laughed lightly as he said, "Yes, as of about an hour ago." Nobody else shared in his attempt at cheerfulness, and instead, the Seer that had been speaking sternly continued without hesitation.

"I will speak straightly with you. We need to know the exact location of one of the primary local offices where some of your former leaders meet regularly. We know they disguise the buildings as to deter us from what they call our "attacks". Your revealing of an area or address where such a building is located will prove to us your commitment to join the Chosen."

"That is no problem at all." Timoria said. "What exactly do you plan on doing to them?"

I had a feeling that Timoria did not trust these men. Thus, if he discovered that they intended on harming someone in the Unenlightened, he would probably give a false address. The heart I had beheld in this man, even over such brief of a time, was of such quality that I suspected that he already knew this truth: that killing those that had killed was vain. In the end, such an act possessed no real justice and did not further our cause. We had come to understand that taking an eye for an eye was a barbaric way to live, immature and carnal, though instinctive. We were learning to rise above such innate reactions, or so I hoped we were.

"We plan on sending "suicide bombers", or so they call them." Said a Seer from somewhere on the left side of the room.

Timoria's face showed obvious disgust, and he began to mouth off a random address in the center of town.

"We know you are lying. Let us explain. What the Unenlightened call bombers involve no real bombs. They are not there to harm anyone, only to preach."

"I don't understand." Said Timoria.

"We send men that are full of such zeal for The Eternal that they are willing to give their lives to burst into a room and preach the truth for a few seconds before they are killed, all to convert just a few leaders, or none at all. What they call suicide bombers, we call roulette preachers, and it is a very dangerous job, with no expectation of survival. We do not deny the name the Unenlightened give these men, because while it is a misleading name, it is also accurate at the same time. When these men break into a room, the light that is upon them is blindingly gorgeous, like the light of an actual explosion. The violence of love they carry could be more accurately compared to a bomb than what you think of when you picture a traditional preacher. Like a bomb strapped to their chest, they are men that willingly go to their death. Their reward is great."

Timoria was taken back, excited about what he was hearing of love rather than murder. "In that case, I will tell you exactly where the headquarters is."

After some time of Timoria explaining details of where the building was and how to access it, the roulette volunteers were sent out, and the Seers moved onto their next order of business.

"Scythe, what we are about to divulge into is of the utmost confidentiality. Do you understand?"

"Yes, my lords."

"Timoria, do we have your word that you will keep what you are about to hear undisclosed?"

"Sure guys."

The way Timoria spoke caught the Seer off guard, as though he interpreted Timoria's words as dishonoring rather than personable warmth that Timoria always spoke with. "Uh...Good." The Seer looked half pleased. "Are you familiar with those that have surfaced over the past years that we call The False?"

"Only some, my lords." I said.

My knowledge of The False was somewhat limited, mainly because I listened and obeyed when the Seers told us to stay far away every time one appeared on the scene of humanity. Their rise was always sudden, as was their inevitable crash-and-burn, like a passing fad. Nonetheless, many were sucked into their deceptive ideas and thoughts during that short stint of time, usually never able to regain any real bearings for truth afterwards.

"We have done well at staying faithful to truth during these times, and always outlasted these falsities when they arose. It is just another way that The Darkness attempts to deceive and seduce us. But this time may be different; a greater challenge." Those present became visually uncomfortable as the Seer said that last part. The room went dead quiet, and the fear that filled the air was hard not to notice.

"My lord, what exactly are you referring to?"

"A new false messiah has arisen."

"A new false *messiah?* This is not the usual false clairvoyant, but a falsely anointed one?"

"Yes, my son."

My heart dropped. False mind readers and diviners had come before, declaring that they were Seers, but for there to be a false *messiah*, though not unheard of, was a much more weighty matter.

"I am sure you know how we have dealt with this in the past." The Seer said to me.

"I do." Timoria interjected.

"Yes, I forgot about that. I am sure you do." The Seer said to my friend.

"I, on the other hand, haven't a clue how you dealt with them." I said.

Timoria turned to me and explained. "At some point, most of the messiahs would make some kind of agreement with us, the Unenlightened, so that they could go about constructing a following without our hindrance. Typically there was some sort of payment that they gave us, such a financial contribution to our organization. They got this money from their followers through collecting money, calling it the people's "tithes and offerings". The coffers were filled and we had our payment, which enabled the messiahs to move about as they wished and do as they pleased, gathering more and more people under their wings."

"So how did that relate to the Counsel of Seers?"

"We desire to protect truth at all costs." Spoke a seer to my right. "You must understand, we are responsible before the Eternal for the spiritual health of those that we shepherd. If they are misled, it is our fault. The Eternal is very gracious and loving, but it is no trifling matter to lead others astray, even in the least bit. I for one will not make that mistake, for I do not want to experience the punishment that would be brought upon one for such an act."

"Thus," spoke another Seer standing directly in front of me, making direct eye contact, "we did what we needed to do in order to protect the Chosen from the lies The False were trying to infect our people with."

"What does that mean exactly?" I asked.

Timoria offered the answer. "It means that the Counsel would contact us."

"What?" I was surprised, even a little bit upset, though I knew that I should not question the Seers. Maybe they knew something I didn't, for they could hear from heaven better than I could. I quickly composed myself and resigned my heart to trust their motives and actions, assuming they had some knowledge that I didn't possess, and if I did I would have made the same decision.

"We would simply communicate to the Unenlightened our distaste for the newly arisen spiritual celebrity. After some negotiating, the Unenlightened would see things from our point of view and would take care of the threat for us. We never had to dirty our hands, and stayed pure before the Eternal. Our goal of purity and holiness were never lost."

I didn't quite understand what the Seers were saying, and I fought off questions that my conscience was bringing to mind. No matter; these were my superiors, I had trusted myself to their care for years, seen many killed for our stand of truth, and they had never led me wrong. So, I sealed up the part of me that was asking questions that I had no answer for. I felt much better when I did.

"In this particular situation, we do not desire to involve the Unenlightened. Instead, we want to send someone to this faction of The False that can possibly persuade this man to our side. We try to be as gentle and gracious as we can at first. If that doesn't produce the intended results, we move on to greater measures. Do you understand?"

I felt that it couldn't have been more unclear. I didn't understand what they were implying. "Are you saying that you want *me* to go to this falsity and attempt to convert him?

"Yes, exactly."

"Why me?"

"Because time and time again we have witnessed your ability to convert those that are the least likely to convert. You have favor with those that do not know the ways of the Chosen. Now, do you accept this proposal?"

Much in this conversation had made me uncomfortable, but all I was being asked to do was go to an unbeliever and convert them. It would be quite a challenge, but I liked challenges of this sort, so I accepted.

"Good. We are sure you will make us proud. We would like you to take Timoria with you, for two are better than one, and the initial twelve were sent out in pairs of two. Go, do the will of He who is sending you."

The bags went back over our heads and we were led up the stairs we had descended. After some time of walking the bags came off, and the sun kissed our faces once again.

We had been given an assignment from The Almighty, and it was time to pursue its execution.

Eight

The next day we left with no real plan. All we had were the coordinates given to us by the Seers of where this heretic's command post would be stationed.

Timoria was just as excited as I was, enlivened by adventure, the unknown, and the threat of danger. If I hadn't encountered divine Love years before, I would have continued happily in my previous profession. Being a sniper had suited me. But after tasting of fruits in gardens Above, I was changed. It wasn't that my profession had grown overtly *evil* to me, but that I simply didn't *enjoy* it like I used to. I had learned that maturity wasn't so much the ability to abstain from desires, but having them changed. I no longer had a hunger to silently hunt, mark, and remove someone from more than a mile away. My need for adventure and risk was more than satisfied in the new "army" I had been drafted into.

Neither of us knew exactly what to expect of this "messiah" or his followers. This didn't deduct from, but added to, our excitement. We hoped for a peaceful interaction, but knew that more dramatic consequences may be a part of our visit. Either way, we had been told by the Seers that our job was to attempt to gain favor with this leader and lead him into the Chosen. If we couldn't do that, would we need to at least show him the errors of his teachings in hopes of repentance. If there was no repentance, the Seers had told us to report back to them and they would handle it from there.

They told us of what they knew about this heretical despot, which was little. It sounded as though this man's teachings were the Seer's main concern, besides the fact that he was calling himself the messiah. The Seers had come to learn that he led a mounting group of people that referred to themselves as The Embrace. The Seers told us that this name could be easily mistaken as perverse, as though it was named without much thought or foresight. It even caused some of our more set-apart leaders to shutter when they spoke it; the name came off their lips with bitterness and distaste the same way we, the Chosen, would speak of sin and rebellion. And from what the Seers had told us of the heretic's teachings, it was no wonder why they felt so strongly about him.

Their complaints were many. They told us that his teachings left him with no real value for justice, appearing to be powerless. That He talked of issues that were black and white as though they were grey. That He didn't preach against sin, and didn't come with the power that they needed.

We all agreed that in such an hour as this, we needed justice. We needed overt, atom-bomb power in order to level the playing field. The injustice that was being dealt out day after day against the widow and orphan, not to mention our own people, was never-ending. If there wasn't justice for the hurting and broken in the teachings this man taught, then, simply said, he wasn't the Messiah. We may not know the hour, but we knew the signs; the Messiah would come and make things right; our salvation from Above. We knew that He would come with the justice and wrath of heaven, uprooting the evil that had taken hold in the world. We knew the Father loved us, and the logical implication to love is a violently defensible intervention when someone was trying to harm His children. We figured the Father would do whatever necessary to keep His children safe. After all, some were too far gone to be saved, too entangled in the infectious sin that had swept the globe years before, right? We had read in the ancient scriptures of accounts where He removed the lives of many heathens on earth in the process of furthering the plans of His people, and we hoped He would be faithful to do it again on our behalf.

The Seers spoke of this man and his movement with distaste because his teachings seemed to frame the Eternal as devoid of any real ability to destroy evil. This was an obvious violation of the signs of the Messiah. We knew there would only be one Messiah, one that came in force on our behalf, and that He would come after many others that were false. With these facts in place, it was easy to deduct that this man was one of the false Seers that would come prior to our savior.

Timoria and I spoke of these things as we walked. As we talked, he repetitively asked the same question in different ways; "But what are the actual teachings this man is giving to others?" I didn't have an answer, and figured we would soon find out for ourselves. We had been told the Seer's conclusions to His teachings, but never the teachings themselves.

Timoria had a way of asking the common sense questions that I never thought to ask. I secretly admired this about him. Some may have called it a rebellious mindset, for the Unenlightened certainly thought so now, and even the

Seers seemed weathered by his many questions when we sat in their company. But I could see that it was this very mindset that had delivered him out of the ranks of the Unenlightened and into my house that dark night, resulting in his redemption. It was as though Timoria's inbuilt way of thinking led him outside of the confines of the box that was given to him, consistently prompting him to ask questions that were astoundingly practical, yet threatening and hard to answer for superiors because they were *real* questions. His wonderings about the Seers and their perception of the heretic was a legitimate point, and caused me to hold back from drawing strong conclusions about the man we were on our way to see until I heard his beliefs from his own mouth.

We walked a long dirt road that ran east and would soon collide with a small town in a few days walk that was our destination. The sun was hot and felt as though it was standing above us, looking down directly upon our frames. I couldn't decide if its rays communicated a motherly care by watching over us, or if it was using everything it had to keep us from walking, almost like it was shaming us and standing in our way.

The heat caused us to take off our shirts, dip them in a nearby stream, and wrap them around our heads to keep us cool. Despite the heat, the setting was nonetheless idyllic as usual. Though man had bombed and destroyed so much of the earth's surface and foliage, it still sprang back with life in countless shades of green. Like kudzu acclimates to its new climate better than its old, resulting in the domination of its new territory despite man's attempted slowing of its growth, creation wouldn't stop exemplifying its beauty even when man burned it back with every fiery warhead he had.

It was the resilience of the ground, its begging for peace, its rebellion to the sins of the land.

We walked past and through vast expanses of land; green fields, tall evergreen forests, and desert like open areas full of rocks and red dirt. Earthquakes were as common as the rainless clouds passing overhead, and we barely flinched anymore when the earth would groan. This had been a regularity for years, as though she were crying out for the pinnacle of creation that lived on her skin to stop destroying each other. She squirmed because we harmed each other, but also because we harmed her in the meantime. It was as though she pleaded with us to mature; for mankind to step into the revealing of their identity.

And the earthquakes were just the start. Because I had been with the Chosen I had forgotten of the judgements that were regularly released upon the earth, for they seemed to pass us over us. Thus, they were not at the forefront of my mind like they were for many, or how they were for myself in the past. Plagues swept over the earth and were said to have killed more than could be counted. Actual mythical beings had (and it was rumored still did) perused the earth, looking for anyone created in the image of the Eternal so that they may remove their imagery from the earth. I had come face to face with one of these beings once, the kind that high school students used to study in greek fiction classes. To recall that moment provides me with the utmost amount of uneasiness, so I would rather not go into it. Summarized, this place had become a nightmare that crept out of the realms of dreams and into our realm of reality. Things were much worse than one could ever imagine.

But oddly, and more importantly, these things never afflicted us (the Chosen) as they did the rest of the population. At first it seemed like random odds, like in war when a grenade goes off in the presence of a group of people and a few live while the others are either killed or wounded. Many thought that it was as arbitrary as roulette who was afflicted and who was not, thus we cowered, but after some time we saw that it was always those that were apart of the Chosen that experienced divine protection. Once we understood this, all fear fled from us and we became very courageous.

This left the Unenlightened to be the ones primarily afflicted by these things. Thus, though it seemed that the Unenlightened had the upper hand (some argued this because they had the majority of the population in their grasp as well as the financial capabilities to finance their plans), the hardships and defense they had to put forth was extraordinary. It seemed that at times they could barely function in their desired goal to dismantle the Chosen because they were fighting on other fronts against enemies that couldn't easily be destroyed. Their enemies were more spirit than flesh, and the weapons of warfare that the Unenlightened possessed didn't do much to dissuade the assailments from these adversaries. The Unenlightened suffered much.

I always thought these beings, and the different types of bucking that the earth dispensed, were a form of justice; a way for the Eternal to remove evil from the earth and defend us. But I have to be honest that when I saw the results of these situations, a corpse here and a orphaned child there, it made my zeal and conviction dissipate quite quickly. I wondered how this heretic would view these apocalyptic realities.

At night Timoria and I slept on our backs and talked of contemplative matters until we fell asleep, inspired by the vast amount of stars tacked up to the black backdrop of the night sky. We woke to the sunrise and the dew of the morning, and rested in the shade of any large trees we could find during the midday. Routinely others going in the same direction on the road by bike, in car, even jogging, passed us. They consisted mostly of single mothers, social misfits, odd non-categorized individuals, sickly looking persons, and the elderly. And after a few days of such a restful saunter together, Timoria and I came upon the town wherein the heretic was rumored to reside within.

Entering town, we asked were the heretic was stationed, but nobody seemed to possess the knowledge of where this man was. The town had a curious feeling of peace about it, like an unseen blanket was draped over it that kept everyone warm and content, even the feeling of safety, the way a person feels when they wake on a winter's morning, wrapped up in bed. There was also a curious feeling of *life* there; the trees, grass, brush, and general flora seemed to be flourishing, though this little town was situated in a desert patch of land that seemed to have little rainfall. In fact, just outside the town, nothing grew. I assumed they had good wells and irrigation; like an oasis in the Sahara.

We continued to ask people of this man, but nobody had any information that helped us, though they genuinely seemed happy to help us. After some time I saw a face that looked vaguely familiar to me. It had been quite some time since I had seen Kyle, and he had grown up, now looking older, more mature, with strong cheekbones and bold eyes. We had gone to many of the same gatherings together in the past, then one day Kyle and his mother and father seemingly disappeared. We had assumed the Unenlightened had detained them for an undisclosed amount of time.

"Kyle, is that you?"

"Scythe?" He exclaimed with delight. "What are you doing here? I thought you lived a few days walk from here."

"I do, but we have come on a special mission given to us from the Seers to find a heretic leader in this town. Are you familiar with such a man?"

"Ah, the Seers. It has been such a long while since I have seen them or the Chosen. I believe I know of the man that you speak of, only because I remember what the Chosen believe. You didn't have any luck in finding Him before because nobody here believes He is a heretic but a great leader. Come, I will take you to where he resides."

Kyle's words didn't console the concerns that were at the forefront of my mind about this man and his followers. I realized that Kyle and his family had been living in this town the whole time, never detained like we had assumed and prayed against. In fact, they had probably fled here without letting the Chosen know, which was strongly disconcerting.

Kyle seemed joyful, walking beside us, reaching up and laying his hand gently on my shoulder every few minutes, as though he was sincerely pleased to see me. I felt loved. I couldn't deny that his presence and touch was thoroughly pleasant, even though my mind was racing with questions as to why he and his family had left the meetings of the Chosen. If he wasn't going to our meetings, was he still in the fold?

Kyle led us up to a small, two-story house that was nestled up against the side of a rock, mountain wall. We climbed the steps to the front door on the first floor, and walked inside.

Nine

The room was exceedingly simple; a waiting room with a secretary seated at a desk at one end of the room. It was quiet and calm inside, with only the sound of a clock ticking on the wall amidst the intermittent scribbling sound that a pen makes when put to paper.

I had imagined a strategic planning office of a militant sort, or at least a political campaign-like setting wherefrom this man could be preparing his next crusade. I had assumed a place full of the hustle and bustle of planning and scheming, but this office had none of the sort. There were no hurried actions like desperate, procrastinating fathers in shopping centers on Christmas Eve. In fact, it didn't seem like anyone was doing *anything*. For a second I found myself chuckling as I stated in my head, "Maybe *I* should volunteer. Then maybe they would get something done around here!"

We sat down in a row of chairs on one side of the room as Kyle approached the desk and asked if we may have some time with the leader. She looked up and smiled as she asked for our names, wondering if we had an appointment.

Kyle looked back at us as he answered, "No, I don't think they have an appointment."

"Well, lets get their names anyways" she replied.

He gave her our names, and again a smile stretched out on her face as she said, "Actually, yes, they do have an appointment. Someone must have called in days ago. There are a few people ahead of them, so they will need to wait, but he will see them soon."

I hadn't called in, so I assumed the Seers had scheduled an appointment. As I was thinking about why they had made an appointment for us, I turned to talk to the man sitting next to me. There were only a few others in the room, all seemed to be waiting to talk to the heretic leader. I figured it was a good time to do some reconnaissance; interview those that had spent time with this heretic in order to gain more information about him.

"Hello. What is your name?" I asked politely. "My name is Richard. How are you?" I told him I was fine, hurriedly trying to end the shallowness that every conversation begins with, and attempting to lead our talk into a more substantial level of thought and depth. I wasn't one to dilly-dally around in conversation. "So what brings you here?" I asked.

"He is the first one to speak about a Higher Power that resonated with my heart." Richard said. Richard was a thin man, glasses resting far down on his nose, the way that causes a person to slant their head downward ever so slightly when they engage you in conversation so that they don't view you through their reading lenses and blur your image. He looked intelligent, well read, even brilliant.

"What in your heart did he resonate with? I asked.

"Well you see, I am an atheist. But the way this man talks of The Designer entices me."

"An atheist? Entices him?" I thought. I assumed that by "The Designer" he meant the The Eternal. What teachings of The Eternal could entice an atheist if they were correct teachings? I may have not heard this heretic's teachings from his own mouth, but no wonder the Seers were concerned! If this man's teachings were luring *atheists*, then what value could they hold?

"Please go on." I said.

"Well, I grew up in a religious home. I must give you some background. Do you have the time?"

"Yes."

"Ok. We attended services every Sunday, I memorized scripture, and regularly fasted. All of that was fine and well until the day my mother suddenly died. I was young, decimated by the loss. The unnerving part was that the Chosen told me that The Designer had taken her life. I didn't understand this because I had been taught that The Designer is love. But they wouldn't relent, telling me that I would find the most peace from the pain of my loss if I surrendered myself to believe that The Designer took her. Strangely enough, my heart wouldn't let me accuse The Designer, or at least the Deity I knew, of such a thing. I was childlike then. Much of the scriptures seemed to say otherwise, or at least the verses the Chosen quoted to me. They told me The Eternal gives and takes away, as though it was His divine joke to give me something so wonderful and desperately needed, then yank it away. They would have never called it a joke, mind you. They would have said there was a purpose and plan in what had happened; a greater reason and love behind what had happened, but that I just didn't have the perspective on it yet. Bollocks to that. What a cop-out.

Let me say as a sidebar that if one desires to, they can quote verses from the Bible that are far more barbaric than any of the statements made in the Koran. Remember that it was Moses that invented the concept of jihad, or holy war, not Mohammad; the destruction of the Canaanites came far before Mohammad was ever born. Am I touching on tender places yet?"

I nodded. Richard paused for a moment as he casually pointed to the door in the back of the room.

"Do not fret, there is an answer. I found it, as you will. And it lies just beyond that door.

Anyways, back to my personal story. My heart wouldn't give in to accusing The Designer of the things that I was seeing in the scriptures and being presented by His followers themselves.

So, my choice was very simple. I could choose to believe that The Designer took my mother and continue to serve that god, the same god that told The Designer's people to "show them no mercy" and was capable of taking life. Or I could choose to believe that if The Designer does exist, He is unable to harm me like that. And because the people that claim to follow The Designer told me that it was He that gave her the disease and took the last, desperately needed breath from her lungs, I chose to believe that there was no god at all rather than believe that the The Designer that I knew had done something so heartlessly cruel. It was the best way I knew how to honor Him at the time.

I surrendered myself to the thought that there was no god rather than to believe that The Designer was capable of wearing a façade of love but in actuality would kill at the drop of a hat, like some of the verses in the scriptures portrayed Him. The convictions deep within my heart, never put there or tended by me but someone else, reasoned that if there *is* a The Designer, He would be loving, with no shadow of turning in Him.

My friend, I will tell you now that the Chosen's theology is a ticking time bomb, waiting to detonate people's faith in the moment something goes utterly wrong."

Something in his words grabbed at me, something subtle and easily missed. It wasn't temptation necessarily, though I thought so at first. It was something I couldn't put a name to, but carried with it a feeling of freedom. I reminded myself that this man was a self-proclaimed atheist, that his words were surely tainted by his off based beliefs and studies, and thus quickly regained my mental composure.

Richard continued, "Over time, my rejection of The Designer, though done out of the purest of motives, even faith, became bitterness. I wanted to prove His lack of existence because the pain of my heart. If He hadn't taken her life, then I wondered why He would allow such a thing to happen if He is sovereign. It became my obsession to prove that The Designer did not exist, instead of proving what I firstly set out to prove; that The Designer didn't do evil things.

My child's heart soon grew into an adult's heart that yearned for the knowledge of man rather than revelation. And the Chosen didn't help steer me back to the right path. On the television the evening news would show this or that natural calamity where thousands would be killed, then The Chosen would say that it was The Designer's doing because of His hatred of sin and need to cleanse the earth for His chosen. And over time, as I observed their teachings, in every vein and stream and flavor in the Chosen (to varying degrees but always present), they would preach that The Designer was capable of taking life. Every time I heard it I grew more and more upset at them and their idiocy, for in my heart of hearts I didn't believe that He did those things, but had no real answer why they *did* happen. Thus, I also grew more bitter towards The Designer, reasoning that if He did exist and if He didn't do those things, why didn't He stand up for Himself and correct His deaf and blind followers that claimed to know Him? But He kept silent, or so it seemed, which added to my growing suspicion that He had never been a reality to begin with, made-up, probably by weak people that needed a mental crutch to lean upon in life.

This went on for years. I now see that I was hunting for truth, but killing the wrong animal. One day I heard of this man, the one you call a heretic, and listened to him. The way He spoke of The Designer was everything that I ever dreamed of. He embodied the hidden beliefs of my heart, and shattered me wide open.

I wouldn't say that I am part of the Chosen, for that word has become a shadow of the substance it should be and I do not wish to be affiliated with those that identify themselves as such, but I definitely admire, love, and follow this man, heretic in the eyes of the Chosen or not."

I didn't know what to say to this confused individual, so I just nodded and faced forward in my chair. This heretic's teachings were drawing in people that *didn't believe in The Eternal.* I was abhorred.

My mind fed over and over again on the same thoughts, like a broken record does sound, and I couldn't get far enough away from them to stay out of earshot. The main repetitious deliberation was; "The Eternal not taking life?" No wonder this leader had been labeled a heretic, for the ancient scriptures *clearly* said otherwise. And I believed the whole book, not just parts of it. Even the mere thought of contradicting the holy scriptures caused anger to rise in me.

At the same time, in a place of me I wasn't even willing to admit to myself by making it conscious, something about what I had just heard allured me. Maybe it was because this heretic's teachings had caused an atheist to acknowledge his belief in The Eternal, however misled he may be. That was some progress, wasn't it? Or was it?

Timoria continued talking to the atheist, excited. I phased out their conversation and began to think of my time with this "leader" and how I would go about convicting him of his theological errors. I would definitely need the scriptures, from which I would highlight verses that teach the opposite of what He is teaching, whatever those teachings turn out to be. I was sure that when He saw that he was contradicting the Word of The Eternal in his teachings, he would relent.

The front door creaked as it was opened by a slender man that walked in and sat a few chairs away from me. Always taking the opportunity to win one to the Chosen, I initiated.

"Hello. How are you today?"

"I am fine, thank you. Is this your first time visiting Him?"

"Yes, it is, if when you say 'him' you mean the man behind those doors."

"Yes, He."

"What is his name anyways? Nobody has given me a real name yet."

"Oh, He will tell you that. No need to tell you now, or you would draw conclusions about Him that will keep you from hearing what He says. Don't worry, my friend. You will enjoy your time with him. Nobody doesn't."

I wanted to let his words calm the growing unrest in my mind, but I couldn't ignore the obvious clues that were solidifying in my head the conclusive fact that I was arriving at. The intentional lisp, the way he waved his hands as he talked, the overall femininity of this man all led me to one conclusion; He "preferred" men over women. I scolded myself for making that assumption until he took off his long sleeved shirt to reveal a pink shirt underneath. On the front of the shirt there was a sketching of Jesus saying, "I love gay people too. Get over it."

I thought to myself, "Sure He does. He loves the person but hates the sin." I felt smug after saying that, like everything was tidy and sorted out, the way you feel after you have given your house a good cleaning.

"So...what is your name?" I asked, while trying to avert my eyes from his shirt, like it hadn't caught my attention.

"Lance. What is yours?"

"Scythe. Nice to meet you, Lance."

I realized that I was having to consciously choose to extend my hand to shake, when usually it shot out in a friendly fashion all on its own. I guess I didn't know where those hands had been, or what death coursed through his veins because of his lifestyle. Simply put; he scared me. We shook hands and I asked him what brought him to the leader.

"I know what you are thinking; Why am I here if I am gay. That is a good question. Simply put, He makes me feel safe. Until I met Him I had never found someone that valued righteousness so deeply, yet abstains from condemning others in their possession of it. He has taught me that righteousness has less to do with what I do than what I believe about myself, and Him."

Righteousness that wasn't related to what we *do*? This sounded like Gnosticism, an age-old heresy! Everything in me wanted to preach the truth to this man right there and then in this room, telling him to repent for his sin, but before I could, he continued.

"It isn't that He has watered any standards down, but I have come to realize that He isn't as concerned about sin as I initially thought. He has communicated to me that He values relationship with me more than cleaning me up. So for now, I am just spending time with Him."

This must have been some of what the Seers warned us about. Lance said that the leader valued righteousness, but that didn't seem to be true. How could he value righteousness if he didn't give attention to sin?

Lance continued. "In fact, He never brings up my lifestyle. He *does* bring up the shame, condemnation, self-hatred, and guilt that I feel, but only to take it away. He never makes me feel bad for what I have done, nor even brings up what I do or have done. Over and over He tells me that He doesn't want to fix me, but love me."

It was all too simplistic and lukewarm for me. Homosexuality was clearly highlighted in the Bible as a sin with deadly consequences, something The Eternal especially hated. If this heretic was treating it with such lax, this too could be added to the list of blasphemies that we would need to confront this man about.

The door to the waiting room opened again, and a striking woman walked through the door, dressed without any modesty at all. You could have caught fish with the stockings that covered her legs, and her short skirt could have made even the most controlled, pure, Seer stumble. Her top left nothing to the imagination, clearly mapping out the curves of her chest and lean stomach. Timoria and I gaped, but the atheist and secretary continued in talking and writing without giving her any more attention than what they had given to us. The woman went to the desk that the secretary sat at, spoke quietly with her, then crossed the room and sat in the chair directly to my left.

"Hello." She said. "My name is Natalia."

"Hello." I said. For all I cared, that could have been the extent of our conversation, for I feared that her mere appearance could lure me into impure thoughts, but she continued.

"What is your name?"

"Scythe"

"Nice to meet you Scythe."

"Thank you. Eh, you too. May I ask you, why you are dressed so....uh, revealingly?"

She laughed. "I wouldn't make any money if I covered up! Customers need to see what they are buying before they purchase the goods."

"But then why are you here? I have been told that this man is a religious and political leader. What would interest you about him?"

"A religious leader? Ha! I think not. And politician? You have to be joking. Administration is his last concern. He says he is here to gather, and there isn't any real plan in place for that anyways. This is as grass roots as you can get. But to answer your question; I am here because I love his company."

"His company?"

"Yes, did I stutter?"

Again, uncomfortable, I sat facing forward in my chair, this time realizing that my hands were gripping the tops of my knees so tightly that my knuckles were turning white from the tension. I needed to relax. The woman had diverted her attention to her cell phone, which made me feel like that I was off the hook in having to carry on a conversation with her.

I normally wouldn't have any problem with evangelizing the atheist or the scantly clad woman, but in this place all of my formulas and methods for conversion didn't seem to fit. I wasn't sure if they thought they were already saved or not. Did I need to evangelize them, or sternly correct their improper beliefs and actions? Evangelizing them when they were already saved would be insulting, and not evangelizing them if they weren't would be a wasted opportunity.

The secretary called for Natalia and she disappeared through a door in the back of the room. Timoria and Richard were still talking, and I prayed that Timoria wouldn't be baited into anything harmful for his newly found faith. After thirty minutes or so, the woman came back out of the door she had entered, blotting her eyes and, I have to admit, glowing with joy. She walked past us as she made her way to the door, and while almost swooning, said, "He is so beautiful. Have a wonderful time with him."

How was I supposed to interpret that? He *obviously* *wasn't* preaching against transgressions or she wouldn't have exited in that fashion, in such joy! If he had rebuked her lifestyle and dress she would have come out with sternness on her face, some sort of visual repentance, maybe even shame and guilt. But there was none of that. Before I could answer the flood of questions proposing themselves in my head, the secretary called for the atheist and he got up and walked through the door that led to the leader.

As soon as the door closed behind him I asked Timoria, "What did you two talk about?"

"The Designer, mostly. Richard is a wonderful man. It seems he has been dealt a bad hand of cards in life, but I think he is still going to win this round. He had a keenness about him that I enjoyed."

"Yes, but what about The Designer did you talk about?"

"It was one of the most enlivening conversations about The Designer that I have ever had with someone. He was telling me some of the things that the Teacher talks about..."

"Wait, what things exactly?" I blurted out.

"Scythe, you will see. He will tell you himself. You don't need to be concerned."

"Easy for you to say. You have been saved for less than a week, what would you know?"

We were both shocked at the impoliteness of my speech. It was as though this little house brought out the worst in me. It reminded me of how the Seers spoke when something came along that interrupted the traditions or agenda that they had. Why was I so raw? Why did I feel a certain feeling of judgment towards everyone else, even a notion of needing to defend myself for no real reason at all? I had felt so much peace before coming into this office, and wondered why I had lost that now. Again, this did not make me anymore excited about the teachings this man had. Every minute I was in this place I became more and more someone I didn't know, or like, like something was being uncovered that had been hidden deep within myself. So far we had tallied up three followers of this man; an atheist, a prostitute, and an active homosexual. His reputation wasn't looking good.

Our name was called, and we walked towards the door that would open to the heretic leader waiting on the other side. We were about to meet the "messiah".

80 | THE COMING

Ten

"Hello my friends!" the man exuberantly bellowed as he gave both of us large, welcoming hugs. His hold was firm and gentle at the same time, wrapping his arms as far around us as their length would permit, leaving me with a feeling that was fatherly, brotherly, and even warm, though I didn't want to admit it.

He was a relatively normal looking man, not overtly handsome, but not unattractive either. I had expected a well-dressed man of stunning stature, one that had the ability to draw people to himself not just through alluring teachings, but also through his physical appearance. This man was nothing like that; dressed mediocre with no outstanding, attention-grabbing suit or of professionalism or garb of religious superiority.

The room was simple, with one chair on one side of the room, and a row of chairs on the other. We seated ourselves, as he sat down in the single chair five or six feet away. The smell in the room was fresh and clean, with scents of vanilla and cinnamon. There were a few windows and a skylight that lit the room well, and a thick, comfortable carpet underfoot.

"Please come in and sit down." His words were spoken with kindness, like a suggestion rather than a command.

"I have been expecting you and looking forward to being with you. It was I that scheduled your appointment a few days ago. That was when you were sent here by the Seers, wasn't it?"

"Yes, it was. How did you know that?"

He leaned in, as he raised an eyebrow and said, "I have many eyes watching from many places", then unexpectedly broke into laughter. He seemed very comfortable. I wasn't.

He went on. "Anyways...the Seers. I love them very much. What a mixed up bunch. Their hearts really do want truth. Their methods of finding it are just outdated. When a well goes dry you dig in a new spot, not wait for rain to fill what use to be useful. Stubborn fellows, aren't they?"

Timoria laughed. I glared back at him, communicating my distaste for his lack of defensiveness towards this "messiah". He needed to keep the walls up; needed to play this game carefully.

The heretic noticed my glare and said, "Scythe, receive peace. Nobody is going to do anything but delight in you here."

I actually felt it. I don't know how to explain it, but when he would speak, it was as though He was creating. When words would leave His mouth they almost became material, like you could handle them if they weren't unseen. I didn't necessarily like the peace that I was experiencing, feeling that it was like vinegar wine on the cross concocted to numb the senses. But unlike the cross, I didn't refuse it. Perhaps it would be more accurate to say that I *couldn't* refuse it. It ambushed me. My back, legs, hands, and arms relaxed, and I found myself exhaling a long breath.

"That is more like it. Now, how can I help you two?"

I spoke. "Well, as you seem to know, the Seers have sent us. We have some questions for you. We are unsure of

your teachings, methods, and general 'ministry' overall."
When I said the word ministry, I held up quotes in the air,
just to let him know we weren't sure what he was doing
could be called ministry.

"I would love to talk through any questions you have.
I am an open book, revealing what I believe to anyone that
truly desires to know."

This was a good start. "Excellent." I said. "Then
maybe we could start now. I wasn't able to bring a Bible with
me, and there are some verses I feel led to bring to your
attention. Could we use one of yours?"

He laughed. "Yes by all means. But that won't do you
much good here."

I was shocked. "Excuse me?"

He was still smiling and laughing, obviously finding
something hilarious about my request to base our
conversation upon the ultimate authority; the Bible.

"I said, that won't do you any good here. I will
explain more on that at a later point, when you are ready.
No need in tipping a sacred cow in your life that you are
going to try to resuscitate. Ugly picture that paints, doesn't
it? No, we will cross that bridge when we come to it." He
continued laughing.

I was no less than appalled. If the Bible isn't held up
as the authoritative Word of The Eternal, then there is no
anchor to keep a person from floating about wherever the
tides of heresy take us, ending in an eventual shipwreck.
These tides had obviously taken hold of this man, simply
because he didn't place the kind of honor and value on the
Bible that he needed to. The Bible was our light in darkness,
making the narrow path clear. Perfect, pure, and every part
completely accurate in Its presentation of the nature of The

Eternal. If the Word of The Eternal isn't revered as it should it be, then everything is lost.

Thus, if the Bible would be of little use in this conversation, then I saw very little use in having the conversation at all. It was beginning to become clear how disturbed this man was. It was true, this man and I were on opposite sides. I sided with those that upheld the Good Book, not heretics that held up their own self-prescribed teachings.

And what was just as disconcerting was that laughter seemed to be his mode of operation. It was slightly irritating to me. No, I need to be honest; very irritating. It was as though he wasn't aware of the seriousness of the situation or the weightiness of the hour, verging on disrespectful. He didn't seem to be concerned about anything at all, even carefree. His joy must have meant that he was either intentional about ignoring the mayhem all around him, all the death, all the sickness, all the oppression, or he didn't care about it to begin with. There needed to be a sobriety that came from the hour, a grievance that was needed in order to honor to those that were suffering. Joy was a part of the Chosen's life, surely, but this man was taking it too far. He was too happy!

Just as these thoughts went through my head, ironically, his laughter settled as turned his attention to Timoria.

"But we have something more important than sacred cows to deal with right now, don't we?"

I looked over and realized Timoria was crying. I had no idea why. Honestly, I was frustrated that he was being emotional rather than being focused on the issues at hand. We had real issues to talk to this false messiah about; not the time to be searching the depths of our heart. We had arguments to make, philosophies to discuss, doctrines to prove, and heresies to confront.

Timoria spoke, "It is just that when I am with you, I can feel what my heart longs for. You know what I have done, don't you?"

The still nameless man nodded. "Yes. I saw every life you took when you were with the Unenlightened. I saw the children beg for their life. I saw the mothers plead with you not to take the life of their husbands. And I saw your lack of mercy." He spoke softly with the gentleness that a mother wields when she holds her baby for the first time, but it cut deep nonetheless, the way truth does. He was not one to water things down.

"But beloved, you don't need to punish yourself for that anymore. Before you were born I saw you do those things, and loved you then. I have always delighted in you, even and especially when you were in sin. My ability to delight in you isn't tampered by your inability to live correctly. Now, you must choose to forgive yourself, for I have already forgiven you."

Timoria wept, even wailed. It's like the man had said the magic words to unlock whatever was sealed up inside Timoria that I hadn't had the insight to see. I didn't understand everything that was happening, but I could see that Timoria was being introduced to a new level of freedom.

The man continued, now in a voice that was more stern than the one he was using before, "Also, I break the power of the words that were spoken over you by those that named you, those from your own spiritual family. Your name is Echelon, not Timoria. Your name was always destined to be Echelon, for I was with you even in the midst of your greatest hour of deception, speaking destiny to you through your name before you ever knew me."

"I am confused", admitted Timoria.

"Well, the Seers desire to serve The Eternal, but many times they forget to monitor their hearts and give the same grace to others that they have experienced from Above. As a result, they can be very critical and ungracious, which was true in your case. They had a hard time receiving you as their own because of your past. When the word "judgment" is pronounced in one of the ancient languages, it sounds like the word "timoria". Thus, this name did not serve you well. You were not created for judgment, but for love. Echelon fits you much better."

"Thank you, sir."

"Oh, no need to be formal. You may call me whatever you need to in order to connect your heart to mine. You had a friend of utmost loyalty when you were young named Joshua, didn't you?"

"Yes, I did."

"Would you like to call me by his name?"

"I would like that very much."

Echelon was crying again. Things were happening on such deep levels of Timoria's (or Echelon's, I was confused with what to call him at this point) heart and so quickly that I couldn't keep up. I figured to some degree it wasn't any of my business anyways, but I felt left out, as though I wasn't in the room, like a third wheel tagging along on a date between two awestruck lovers.

I was torn. On the one hand, I had many concerns about this man. He obviously had some kind of demonic gift of insight, and his values, followers, and teachings were all wrong. On the other, the results he was getting, at least with Timoria, were impressive. The healing of Timoria's heart that was taking place before me was beautiful, but I was also thrown off by the authority this man assumed to have. He *renamed* Timoria, essentially overriding the Seer's actions. His words seemed extremely arrogant, but he didn't carry himself in a way that was prideful.

Then he turned to me, smiled as though he really liked me, and handed me the Bible that I had asked for. I turned the pages like someone loading a gun, readying myself to fire away. Joshua sat back and calmly waited for the first bullet to fly.

Eleven

The room was quiet as a light measure of anticipation filled the air. I assume the suspense came because of the questions I was about to ask, questions based in truths clearly outlined in the holy scriptures, and questions that couldn't be negated around or loopholed through. I thought to myself, "Maybe Joshua is even a bit nervous. He should be." I pictured a wolf being cornered by a few sheep; its surrender, their victory, and smiled.

"I suppose we can start with what some of your followers seem to believe, such as the man in the waiting room named Richard." I said.

"Ah, you met Richard! Delightful fellow, isn't he?"

Echelon and I synonymously responded at the same time; He with "Yes!" and myself with "Well..." I looked at Echelon with disapproval again. It felt like one of those moments when a mother asks a question of two brothers that she suspects have stolen some cookies, and they both answer at the same time with different answers, revealing the discrepancy between them.

Joshua laughed, "Yes, I imagine that he was very honest with you. Probably tweaked you a bit, yes?"

"If 'tweaked' means that his beliefs seemed very dishonorable to the scriptures, then yes, I suppose so."

"Scythe, I know you think he was being dishonoring to the scriptures, but that is not his intention. He prioritizes honoring The Eternal over honoring the scriptures. In fact, in assuming the best about The Eternal he is honoring the scriptures in a way that is greater than memorizing the entire book and quoting portions of it at every vaguely applicable moment. For a while there, Richard threw the baby out with the bath water, but he knows that now. I know it sounds peculiar, but Richard was seeking The Eternal in believing that The Eternal didn't exist. I would rather have someone choose to not believe in The Eternal because the example given to them is less than perfect, than have a religious devotee that consciously believes evil about The Eternal but is blinded to it. At least the first will receive Him when He is revealed as He is; good. The other will reject Him because He will not look the way as they have always assumed; good. It makes no real logical sense, but the goodness of the Father is the stumbling block of the ages. In Richard's honoring of the nature of The Eternal, he was honoring the scriptures as well."

"I do not agree. If a person desires to honor the Eternal, they will honor His words and what the scriptures say about His nature, without picking and choosing what they want to leave and take out about Him."

"Ah, yes. But what if there was a greater revelation of who the Eternal is than what is presented of Him in the scriptures?"

"If such a thing *did* actually exist, then logically I would look to that source of revelation for guidance. But such a thing does not exist."

"Wonderful! Then we will have no troubles at all. That source of revelation will become clearer and clearer to you as time goes on."

"I am doubtful of that. The Chosen has never taught of this new "source" of revelation."

"They have, but they haven't known it. Lets move on. What are your thoughts on Richard's dilemma of losing his mother?"

"It is very sad. But I have to say that scripture clearly shows that The Eternal takes life."

"Really? But what of the words, 'The enemy comes to steal, kill, and destroy. I have come that they may have life, and have it abundantly.'"

I paused. "Well yes, but what about Job?"

"That He gives and takes away? That is true; He gives life and takes away sickness and death! What if Job's statement was one of declarative faith rather than a lamentation of sacrificial praise? What if he was saying, "The Eternal only does good things, and I will believe that in the face of horrible things happening in my life. I know He has not done this, thus, blessed be the name of the Lord."

"I had never thought of it that way."

"Most people don't."

"Yet, I have to say, I don't feel that fully answers the heart of my question pertaining to that book though."

"True. The answer you seek lies in me showing you how to view the ancient writings, if you let me. I promise, I won't stretch things or read things into the text that aren't there. There is a Truth that can help turn all of your questions into answers, especially the questions that arise from the ancient texts. This is what Richard discovered."

"I am open to hear about it. In the meantime, can I ask you that if The Eternal didn't take his mother, and the enemy was the one responsible, then what of The Eternal's sovereignty?"

Joshua smiled. "If you believe that everything that happens is the Eternal's doing, then you have to believe that everything that happens is the Eternal's doing." He paused, accentuating his point without the use of words, then continued. "Abortions become the will of The Eternal, as do diseases, starvation, natural disasters, wars, and attacks from the Unenlightened. The list goes on and on. Don't misunderstand me, the Eternal *is* sovereign, I have personally seen it, just not in the way you think."

"Then how?" I said.

"Complete control and complete authority are two totally different issues. A policeman standing on a corner in traffic has complete authority, but not total control. People can still speed if they want to. The Eternal has given everyone the ability to make their own choices, for He does not work through control. The result is that some people speed."

"But how does that relate to Richard's mother?"

"Because when people have the ability to choose to do what is wrong rather than what is right, then they have the ability to invite the enemy into the world to do what he does best; destroy. This is what happened in the beginning. Darkness was not allowed in by the Eternal, but man opened the door to his entrance through sin. Man had all dominion on earth, given to him by the Eternal, but surrendered it to the enemy when he willfully walked his own path."

"But why would the Eternal tempt them with a tree if He knew they would partake of its fruit?"

"Richard asked the same question. The Eternal *had* to put a tree there, for the tree represented *choice*. Without choice there can be no love. Without choice you cannot have freedom, and freedom is the only context in which love can exist. The Eternal wanted people that could choose Him out of love, not because they were robots programmed to love Him. The tree, even though it was our downfall, is one of the greatest symbols of His love, and His desire for genuine relationship."

"Interesting view. So now the enemy has dominion of earth?"

"In a sense, yes. The Eternal still owns the earth, but the management of it is up to us. Long ago, One was sent to buy back the authority that had been lost in the garden, and those that receive Him carry the dominion that He bought. Thus, while the enemy may be managing the earth and therefore reeking havoc at every chance he gets, the Eternal's people are slowly, and peacefully I might add, taking back what is rightfully theirs."

"So you are saying that Richard's mother was not taken by the Eternal, but the enemy?"

"Exactly. This is why Richard loves to be with me. I do not accuse the Eternal of things He has not done."

"I get that. But if He did not do it, then why did He allow the enemy to do it?"

"Again, this stems from a misunderstanding of the Eternal's sovereignty. The policeman in traffic isn't allowing anyone to speed; they are speeding without his consent. Again, having all authority doesn't mean having control."

"But that makes the Eternal powerless."

"Does it? In reality, it makes *you* powerful. He has entrusted you with changing the world with the power He has provided you with. He already did His part. This isn't about the Eternal's inability to move on your behalf, but that He has given *you* all the authority you need to change any circumstance on earth that was constructed by the enemy. The lack is never on His end. Heaven only moves through the hands, feet, and mouths of those that will one day see it.

Anything can present itself and you will overcome it, like the child that was shot on the stage a short while ago."

"How do you know about that?" I blurted, as though I was angry that Joshua, a stranger, knew something about me that was so personal and wonderful. Maybe I felt that way because his detailed knowledge about my life made me vulnerable.

"I told you before, I have eyes everywhere!" The laughter started again, and this time I was a bit more thankful for it. The conversation had caused me to grow tense, gripping the armrest of the chair so tightly that once again, my knuckles had gone white. The laughter soothed me and made me relax, causing me to become aware of the soreness of my right hand that was caused by my death grip.

Joshua reached over and grabbed my hand as he said, "Scythe, I really like you. You have a wonderful heart that is hungry for the truth. I enjoy talking to you."

His words made me uncomfortable, maybe because I questioned if he was trying to manipulate my emotions like someone trying to sell carpet cleaner that compliments you while standing in your doorway. Conversely, maybe his words made me uncomfortable because it seemed like he really meant what he said. I didn't like either scenario.

The hand he grabbed now felt strong and free from pain. This meant nothing to me. I had seen many false Seers work signs and wonders before, and what had happened with my hand could barely be deemed a miracle anyways.

"Thank you. Moving on. Richard seems to believe that the Eternal is incapable of taking life. Is this what you believe?"

"Yes, it is."

"Wow. Thank you for not bobbing and weaving that question. This must have been one of the Seers main concerns."

"Yes, I am sure it is. Tell me, why do *you* think that is a bad thing?" Joshua asked.

"Because in believing and teaching that, you are either admitting that you haven't read the scriptures, or that you don't believe the scriptures. In addition, in teaching that to others, you are leading them astray. The scriptures say that teachers incur a more severe judgment. The Eternal will surely judge you for your teachings, thus I am here to help that from happening by revealing truth to you. You are my brother and I love you, regardless of how much I do not agree with you."

Joshua lifted an eyebrow as if to say, "Do you *really* believe that?" I wasn't sure if I did believe that I would be able to bring him onto the narrow path, but I was sure going to still try.

"Time to step it up. Scythe, during our times together there will be times when I speak very directly, clearly, and simply to you. This is one of those times. I am going to tell you something now that you may not like at all. Fair warning, ok?"

"Nothing could shock me at this point."

Joshua let out a hearty laugh. "I think you will find that is not true."

"Have at it."

"Here it is; what I say about the Eternal is more important than what you surmise from your reading of the scriptures."

"What? Excuse me? Did I hear you correctly?" I said calmly.

"You did. My words trump the words that are written in that wonderful book. If you listen to what I say, you will never be deceived."

"Sir, you are the one that is deceived. And I make it my goal for you to see your deception. Let us pray.

Father, open this man's eyes. Let him see the truth, and have mercy on him in the midst of his confusion. But Father, if he does not relent in his falsities, let your judgment fall upon him for the purpose of his redemption. If you have to take his life for the purpose of saving it, please do for the sake of mercy. Amen."

I opened my eyes to see Echelon and Joshua sitting quietly, looking almost embarrassed, like someone had just ran through the room streaking. They didn't say "Amen" with me and just sat with their eyes open, staring at me rather than respectfully closing their eyes and bowing their heads.

After a few seconds Joshua broke the silence with a quiet chuckle. Typical. Echelon joined in with him, both quickly escalating in the volume of their laughter. The sound and look of it was unavoidably infectious and I even found myself laughing, to my surprise. Joy is like that.

I knew they were laughing at me, but oddly, I didn't feel like their laughter had to do with them making fun of me. Joshua wasn't in the least bit condescending, even when he was laughing *at* me. I felt as though he was delighting in me, not mocking me.

I kept this actuality in the depths of my heart, like a secret, even almost hidden from myself. Maybe I did that because I was afraid to admit how he made me feel. If he was a heretic as he appeared to be, liking him would just make what I had been sent here to do even harder. I needed to correct and rebuke him, convert him, and draw him back into truth. And so far, it wasn't happening like I had expected.

98 | THE COMING

Twelve

e had fatigued the topics we had been conversing about, and our talk had come to a pausing point. Echelon broke the quiet with, "Wow. I am exhausted."

"Yes, talks like that will exhaust a person, plus you also just spent a few days walking here." Joshua said. "Tell you what. How about you two follow me. I have a place for you to stay tonight. I firmly believe in rest, and you guys could use a large dose of it. After you awake tomorrow, perhaps we could spend some time together. Does that suit you?"

We agreed, and the three of us filed out of the room then made our way out of the building. Joshua walked in front of us, leading us down a narrow cobblestone path that cut and weaved through a luscious garden. The smell of flowers and fruits filled the air, intoxicating my senses. The smells and colors were stronger in this garden, as though they had been fed the most concentrated fertilizer ever created.

Then I saw it. As Joshua walked in front of us I watched the heads of the flowers literally follow him and move, staring at him as he walked by. It was as though they stared at him in awe, the way a man watches a woman he secretly loves as she moves past him, moments before he approaches her and asks her hand in a waltz.

I had heard of this before with sunflowers and other plants; the way they would open to the sun and follow it across the sky, but that was movement that couldn't be traced or seen with the naked eye because its speed was so slow. This was different altogether. I watched with wide eyes as the vines that wove between the cobblestone bricks literally reached up and attempted to touch Joshua's feet as he walked by. They didn't move in a way that showed a desire to trip him or get in his way but as though they just wanted to get one brief touch in before his foot lifted again. It reminded me of how people used to treat movie and rock stars when they walked through crowds; reaching out for one fleeting moment of physical contact. These plants made him look famous.

I had seen a lot of scams in the past that appeared to be supernatural but weren't, yet I had never seen a charlatan pull off a trick as stupendous as this. This was either a stunt of incredible proportions, or there was something to this man of great evil or great good. Either way, I was nonetheless spellbound by it.

The path weaved back and forth until it came upon a beautiful house nestled in the midst of the garden. This cabin was constructed of stone and bamboo, fully surrounded by green, like it was going to be swallowed up at any moment by all the life and beauty around it. The chimney spouted white smoke which would have made anyone looking at it feel warm inside. Large windows lined the house, and even while standing outside you could tell that light flooded the inside. To say the least, this house was spectacular.

Joshua climbed the steps to the porch and opened the door for us to enter. It was comfortable and extravagant inside. I immediately felt guilty for staying somewhere so nice when many of the people I loved didn't even have a bed to sleep in some nights.

As if he heard what I was thinking, Joshua said, "Just enjoy yourself Scythe. I love the way you love others, but you need rest now. Just receive this place as a gift. Eat anything and everything you want. I will see you both tomorrow. Sleep well."

We thanked him and he closed the door. I watched him walk back through the garden, with his fans following him the best they could without uprooting themselves and walking after him. The sun seemed to go with him, setting behind him on the horizon and turning the sky a myriad of colors. I couldn't help but feel a bit of loneliness as he left, even sadness. Who was this man? How did he take affect on my heart like this? How and why did creation bow to him?

Delicacies of the utmost rarity, our specific favorites, had been laid out for us in the kitchen, prepared the way we liked it, like someone from our favorite restaurant had called us before time and taken our order. It felt surreal. We were being spoiled, treated like royalty, and we had come to disprove this man. There was no question who was doing better at loving the other party, and it convicted me. Echelon and I spoke little, ate our fill, then made our way to our bedrooms upstairs and slept sound.

I awoke early, refreshed. Euphoric dreams had escorted me through my sleep, and I felt life inside. The smell of cedar was the first sensation I recognized. With the light filling the room I could see why; the entire room was either constructed of cedar boards, or glass. The room consisted of two inner walls of cedar and two completely glass walls that overlooked the garden below. The room was essentially a window that could be inhabited. I stayed there for a very long time, looking out over the sea of green below. The room felt both safe and comfortable while totally transparent, the same way the look that came from Joshua's eyes made me feel.

I made my way to the bathroom that joined the bedroom and showered. I hadn't had a warm shower in months. Water wasn't in abundance usually, let alone warm water, so this was quite a treat. The shower was made of stone, with the showerhead too high above my head to reach it. It spilled out great amounts of water over me, and I relished every drop. There is something about water washing over your body that makes even the spirit feel clean. My whole being relaxed even more, and I soaked there for a long time, letting my sore legs and feet drink of the warmth. After ample time there, I got out, dried, dressed, and went downstairs to find Echelon so that we could continue in our quest.

After breakfast, we went out to the garden path and began the walk to Joshua's office. I admit that I watched the flowers to see if they would follow me with their eyes like they did for Joshua, and to my surprise, a few did. Maybe it wasn't so much Joshua that was phenomenal, but the flowers themselves. I couldn't help but to slightly misuse my newly found power by moving up and down the path, causing the few flowers that gave me their attention to sway their heads back and forth like they were keeping beat to a unheard song. Echelon and I laughed at their movements, and soon we were at the office. Joshua was standing outside waiting for us, smiling.

"I see you have been introduced to our admirers."

"Yes, they are very peculiar. Why do the flowers in this garden move when others do not?" I asked.

"The cabin you stayed in is my own, and I walk down that path past them almost everyday. Thus, they have been near me. I would even go to the extent of saying that they *know* me, for being near me develops into knowing me. The result is supernatural life. This is the way all of creation acted before the day in the first garden. Everything was created with life, free from the stillness that comes before death."

"You are saying that they move because of your presence?"

"Yes."

I paused and thought for a second, lining up a logical statement to undermine what Joshua had just said. "But some of them moved for me as well. I will admit not all of them watched me like they did for you, but nonetheless, if they move because of you, then why did they move for me?" My comment made me feel smug, like one feels after making an insightfully sarcastic and dishonoring comment on a social networking website.

Joshua smiled. "Because they recognize the glory in you. I brought them to life, but now they will respond to anything or anyone that carries the essence of goodness."

I was frustrated and humbled. Even when I was being cocky and presumptuous, his response was honoring and courteous towards me. The best way to dismantle pride is to lavish grace upon the arrogant. I felt taken apart by his graciousness in the midst of my condescension, and the result was unavoidable; I felt loved.

Then he shattered everything I was feeling by adding one more comment. "They respond to me in you."

I cringed from confusion and offense as he smiled like he knew that he had just threw me for a loop. He really did think he was the messiah. He turned and led us up to his office where we sat down to have another "talk". I hoped that this one would go better than our last.

Thirteen

"Now are the two of you? Did you sleep well?" Joshua asked.

We both felt well, and communicated our thanks for having us in his house. I had no idea where he had stayed last night, but Joshua looked rested so I didn't ask.

"Well, what would you two like to talk about today?"

I remembered Lance and Natalia, the gay man and the attractive woman that were in the waiting room from the day before.

"Lets talk about Lance, the man in the waiting room yesterday."

"I would love to! Lance is such a beautiful lover of mine."

"Excuse me?" I said.

Joshua erupted in laughter. "No, not in that way. Scythe, things aren't as perverse as you assume they are. Just relax; everything will go much more smoothly if you aren't so uptight. Remember that to the pure everything is pure."

He was right. I had learned that it was usually those in witchcraft that accused others of it, the perverse that mistake purity as perversion, and the blameless that see the guilty as innocent. We perceive the world through who we are. I was convicted, but regained my composure because I still had questions.

"Lance said that when you two spend time together you don't try to fix him, but just love him. I found this curious. Wouldn't loving him look like getting him to cease his homosexual lifestyle?"

"No, it wouldn't. If he comes to the place of wanting to change his lifestyle, fine. My job has always been, and always will be, to love people right where they are. My love doesn't have an agenda. Lance's lifestyle doesn't lessen my ability to delight in him in the least bit. If he changed his lifestyle tomorrow it wouldn't affect how I treat him at all. My highest priority isn't to change people but to love people. If there is a shift needed in order to maximize Lance's overall happiness in life, rest assured that my love will naturally bring that about, without him trying to make it happen through the force of his own will or the clenching of his teeth. Simply said, my love sorts everything out. The problem is when people try to change others, or when they love others in order to change them. Then when the change they want to see doesn't unfold, they become frustrated and begin to resort to condemnation in order to bring about the modification. And that never works in the long run."

"That sounds like greasy grace to me. I believe that without preaching the need for repentance we lead people to hell."

"Interesting. Repentance is the changing of how one thinks, being refocused on the Above. In turn the actions change and turn away from what first caught their attention. You are saying that you think that bringing a person to a genuine changing of their mind comes through instilling fear into a person instead of loving them?"

"No, I believe that loving them means speaking the truth to them about their circumstances and where they lead."

"Ah." Joshua sat back and looked pleased. "So you are saying that repentance should be preached before love? I believe that love leads to repentance. It is my gentleness that draws the heart of man. See, despite what you have assumed Scythe, this is something that Lance can't make a decision not to feel, at least not for now. These desires come to him as instinctively as hunger does to you and me. You need to understand this in order to be able to impart grace to Lance. This need he has in his heart is overwhelming and insatiable, thus he finds himself staving at times and stumbles into a binge, even if he is attempting to live a "fasted" lifestyle. Lately though, he has learned to binge on me, and the more he does that, the more it fills this driving need. Everything humans do, everything, is driven by a need for love. Lance is no different."

"So what exactly does it look like when he 'binges' on you?" I asked.

Joshua laughed as he said, "Lets just say that there is a reason why I have a lock on the door to my counseling room."

"What?"

"Well, if you were to walk in on one of our sessions, you would likely make warped assumptions about the both of us that are not true. Simply said, I get very close to Lance when we are together. I hold him... I even kiss him." As he said that last bit, Joshua made the sound of a gasp and left his mouth gaping open as he brought his hands up to his cheek with a fake expression of surprise on his face, obviously mocking anyone that would frown on what he was doing. He obviously didn't care in the least bit what anyone else thought about his "counseling methods".

"I know you may not like that Scythe; it probably doesn't seem very professional to you. But the mistake people make with homosexuals is to not be close. The very thing The Chosen are scared to do with homosexuals is the very thing that begins to bring life and closure to their heart; physical affection. The Chosen fear that their actions will be misconstrued and misunderstood. Sadly, they choose to hold others at arms length, and simply talk them through something that cannot be talked away, but touched away. The Chosen do not need to fear that their actions will be misunderstood, but rather just love abandonedly, and leave the rest up to the Eternal."

"This is all very uncomfortable to me." I said.

"I can see that. The good news is that Lance is learning to replace my love with that which has fed him for years. It can take time, like someone who has lived on IVs for years switching back to food. Thus, I am patient with Lance in his focusing back on The Above."

"But that won't slap reality into him though. He needs to know where his actions are going to take him."

"Oh." Joshua sighed. "So you are saying that homosexuals will burn in hell?"

"I wouldn't say it like *that*. But the scripture is very clear about how The Eternal feels about that sin."

Joshua shrugged. "Yeah, I suppose it is." Then he leaned in and lowered his voice, as though he was telling us a secret. "I will tell you something that the scriptures do not say about homosexuality."

"Which is what?"

"That it is no worse to me then the little white lies that every person has told. You have to understand; there isn't a spectrum of evil, ranging from a serious violation to a minor infraction, that people's actions are ordered into by Heaven. And because of that, Lance's lifestyle is no different from yours."

His words pricked my pride, but in a way that felt helpful, not intentionally hurtful. I didn't like how Joshua was always leveling the playing field, but he was right.

"Scythe, I refuse to condemn men. It just isn't in me to do. That position has already been filled by the law anyways, so why have two doing the job that one is doing adequately?" He smiled, then continued.

"In fact, I'm not concerned with sin like you are. It has already been taken care of. The Eternal doesn't have a reason to destroy people for sin. This may be hard to hear, but He does not punish his children, whether they know Him or not.

It isn't much different in Natalia's case. What may shock you even more is that I prefer being with Lance, Natalia, and Richard over dignified, religious, moral people. In all honesty, I find that utterly boring! Their souls have forgotten the color that I once splashed them with. They aren't themselves any more, boxed in and muted to such a degree that they have forgotten what freedom tastes and smells like. Don't misunderstand me, I love them very much, at least the faint whisper of what is left of themselves in that state. Anyways, back to Natalia."

"Yes." I said. "She was quite racy. I even had to advert my eyes as she bent over when she signed in at the front desk because her skirt wasn't doing its job!"

"I know you did. But there is a way to look at a woman that will not cause you to think of her in a dishonoring way, but a way that causes genuine love to well up in your heart for her. That is what I do. I look at her and remember all the men that let her down in her past; all the men that let her down every night. I think about her desperate venture of trying to find a masculine love that won't take from her, a journey she has been on since the day she was born. I think of her two children that she provides for by selling herself to men that she hates, and in doing so reveals her love as a mother and the sacrifice she makes for their well-being.

There is much good to credit Natalia. See, I choose to see her as she is; a good person. In fact, an extraordinary person. This isn't pity; I truly think she is amazing. Pity never helped anyone. What people need is for us to give them dignity, to see them as they want to be seen in all of their love and failures, then for us to embrace the whole of them.

In reality, I am not concerned with changing her lifestyle. I am concerned with her knowing she is wholly loved by me just as she is. The things she does to provide for her family may cut off her ability to receive my love, but I never stop loving her or enjoying her. The only thing that stops the flow of my life is that she sometimes hesitates from receiving it, as is true in anyone's case. People's actions keep their hearts from receiving the depths of delight that I feel towards them. Sin numbs the heart's ability to receive the oxygen it needs; love. Shame and guilt are the real culprits, not even the sin itself. Thus, I just hammer the door of her heart with love until shame and guilt cannot block the way anymore and I am given entrance. Love, true affection, provides an atmosphere in which shame and guilt cannot survive in.

Natalia was given physical beauty, and it is the only way she knows how to provide for herself and her two little girls. But her situation will change. She has encountered a masculine love in me that will not take from her, and over time that will cause her to love herself. The result will be getting a new job, one that will not degrade her as this one does."

Echelon and I were quiet, taking everything in that Joshua was telling us. And as if he knew that we had taken in as much as we were able to in a day, Joshua said,

"That is enough talk for today. Our conversations seemed to be plagued with a fair level of seriousness, and it is not good for anyone to stay in that state for long. There is a party today. We try to host one at least once a week. That should effectively break the sobriety that our conversations have lingered in, at least for some time." Again laughing, he got up and walked out of the room.

I surmised that we were to follow him, so we did.

Fourteen

*J*oshua led us through the town to a field about a mile away. As we passed through town, I noticed that there were no children playing on the streets and shops were closed though it was relatively early in the day. We spotted the field in the distance and I noticed that on one side of the stretch of grass was a stage. A band was already playing on it, and many droves of people were draped across the field, all waiting for the main attraction.

To my surprise, the main attraction happened to be Joshua. I only realized this after he walked up on the stage and the crowd went absolutely crazy, like the Beatles had just made a surprise appearance after decades.

It dawned on me how spoiled I had been to be able to have spent so much one-on-one time with Joshua. It was apparent that many people would have loved to have the time with him that I had. I had not only been able to talk with him, but to touch him and sleep in his home. Though he was a heretic, I felt honored. I was softened by the fact that he made no mention of how desired and wanted he was by many, and yet spent time with me; one who didn't value my time with him like the many people would have that were clawing at the stage to simply touch his feet. I had only dishonored him and argued with him, yet he seemed to enjoy our time together anyways, spending his time with a mediocre adversary rather than fans. Perhaps he cared for me despite how much I disapproved of him.

When the crowd had spotted Joshua, every person went running in the direction of the stage. Sheer madness followed. It was a frenzy, as though Joshua was food and they were just getting off a forty-day fast. The stage started to creek and lean from the weight of the bodies pressing up against it, and it didn't look as though it would hold for long. I thought about rushing out on the stage to warn Joshua, but before I could it gave way. Joshua must have anticipated it, for moments before it was flattened to the ground he leapt off the stage into the midst of them. He never hit the ground, but twenty-some people eagerly caught him, then held him above their heads. I wondered if he jumped from the collapsing stage because he had to, or if he did just because he wanted to. It looked fun, plus he was closer to the people now, so I figured it was probably the latter. I smiled.

The crowd threw him back and forth, gently catching him and passing him all over the field, like they were sharing him with one another. I realized a practical aspect to what was going on that I had missed; it was too hard for the people to get to him so he was going to them.

Then I began to notice shouting that would come from any section of the crowd where he would be passed. It took me a few minutes to piece it all together, but the crowd seemed to be passing him to those that were fatally ill in the crowd, letting him graze over them. Moments after he was passed away from a certain area of the crowd, the ill were springing to health, and the crowd would shout with joy.

Joshua was laughing and laughing as he was passed around, apparently delighting in the healings, the touch of those below him, and especially adoring the recurrent tickling that some would bestow upon his sides. Joshua wasn't uncomfortable with it in the least bit. And oddly enough, it felt like praise to me. In that moment I realized that tickling from a stranger is misconduct, but from someone of close relationship it is a form of intimacy. Joshua must truly know these individuals, I thought.

Soon he was passed back up to the shattered stage, and stood on the leftover wreckage. Echelon and I were standing behind him, and before he addressed the crowd, he looked back at us and said, "Welcome to The Embrace. These are my people. They range from those that I have known for many years to those that I haven't met at all yet."

He turned back to the crowd and said, "Peace and joy be yours. You are loved!" The roar that followed was literally deafening. It was like they had just told them that each one of them had won the lottery. I almost made a joke to Joshua that I needed prayer for my ears, but he was busy with the crowd.

Joshua began to call out physical problems that people had in the crowd. He would then command the ailment to be healed, and it was. He never raised his voice, yet every ear could hear him, though the crowd easily stretched out to over 400 yards away. Every person whose sickness or deformity that he named was made new. None were passed over.

We had seen many miracles in the past during our gatherings with The Chosen. But this was different. It wasn't that there was necessarily a higher number or more dramatic healings when Joshua worked his magic than in gatherings I had attended in the past, but the way they came was different. We had miracles happen *to* us; this man *made* them happen. To some degree, we *waited* for miracles to happen, but this man *worked* miracles. It was as though we waited for a source of power to move on those sick in our ranks, but this man acted as though he *was* the source. It confounded me. There was an unmistakeable feeling of authority in the air, probably not unlike the undercurrent at the end of a gladiator match when the masses waited for the inevitable thumbs up or down from the emperor. In this case, it wasn't a life but disease and deformity that were under the blade, and all agreed for their slaughter. Joshua was quick to drop his thumb south.

And all of this happened in the most disorderly atmosphere (or so we would have called it in The Chosen). If The Chosen's gatherings could be described as reverent and worshipful, this gathering of The Embrace could be described as untamed bliss. It looked more like Woodstock than a religious service. The people looked otherworldly, like their blood ran rich with something akin to hallucinogenic substances. In reality, later I would learn that this was the effect that Joshua had on a heart that received him with no reservations.

Many were being healed and as they were, or even if someone simply witnessed another person be healed, they would involuntarily begin to shout this profession out loud:

"I give myself to this embrace. This is all I desire."

This statement started with ten or so people speaking it out at a time. Soon the entire crowd was chanting it over and over. Joshua looked pleased. As they chanted, Joshua took a few steps back and stood next to us.

"The Chosen began experiencing physical healing long ago, but I draw in people that had never been to their gatherings where healing was poured out. I target a different crowd."

"Yes, you do." Echelon said.

"Scythe, you have wondered if I lack a value for justice. Is this true?" Joshua asked.

"Yes."

He nailed it. I felt this way for many reasons. From his interaction with the people in his office, it seemed clear to me that he seemed unconcerned about sin. Sin brings punishment, and punishment rights the scales, which is one way to describe justice. Thus if there was a lax attitude towards sin and no true value for righteousness, the logical implication was that there was no value for justice! Also, he said that The Eternal was one that wouldn't take life, which means that he believed The Eternal wouldn't destroy evil when He encountered it. If he had a god that wouldn't take life at some point, then there wasn't a place for justice to be manifested against evil! It seemed that if The Eternal was one to sit back and allow another to harm His children through not bringing justice, then logically, that wasn't love. A god that doesn't violently defend His wife or children wasn't a good god at all! I wondered how Joshua would slither out of this conundrum.

Joshua answered, "What you are seeing now is a demonstration of my value for justice. Justice is more about restoration than it is about punishment. Justice comes not through the punishment of one that committed the wrong, but through the healing of the one that was harmed. It is true that two wrongs do not make a right.

Man does not possess supernatural capabilities in and of himself, thus the only ability he has is to punish the one that wronged, even take their life, and compensate the one that was wronged, usually monetarily.

But what I do is forgive the one that violated, and heal the one that was violated. I have no need to take life, only give it. What good would it do to cause more pain? It is not that I don't value justice, but that my justice looks different from yours. My justice has no need to involve punishment. When justice must involve punishment it is incomplete, not yet free from the patterns of the law set forth long ago. I expect this incomplete form of justice from those that do not know me, but not from my own. This is why you need to change your concept of justice. You now know that justice is not related to anger, wrath, or destruction, but love and forgiveness."

Joshua turned back to the crowd that was still chanting the profession of The Embrace. Slowly, the chant became a song. The song began to take on a physical manifestation in the air, the way water when heated, begins to drift into the air. There was a glow that was rising up from the tangled bodies, filling the air and warming my skin. It was unavoidably beautiful, like liquid fire resting in the air.

I felt the hearts of these people burning. They had something I hadn't witnessed before. They didn't just have dedication, duty, or commitment, but a burning that only comes from one thing: passion.

Fifteen

*T*he song waned, and Joshua spoke for a short time afterwards. After speaking, he again started calling out the physical ailments of those that had just arrived, as the crowd was continually growing. More people were healed, and as restorations were taking place, I saw that the band was setting up on the decrepit stage, for the collapse had caused all their instruments to be strewn all over. Joshua wrapped up, pointed at the band, and they started to play. In response, the entire field of people broke out in undignified dance.

I decided to make my way off the stage and join the mass. Immediately I was swept into a dance with a woman who I had never met before. She linked arms with me and we spun in circles. It all seemed so silly and happy. And I confess; I loved it. There wasn't one depressed person in our midst.

Most songs were fast, but there were some songs that were slow wherein we would find a partner and hold them close, man or woman. The level of familiarity we had with each other, though we were strangers, was something to take note of. Things never felt impure, even when I was face to face with a beautiful woman that I can honestly say that I was very much attracted to. It was as though the atmosphere wouldn't allow for us to want anything but the Eternal, or Joshua in the case of The Embrace.

During these slow songs, Joshua would dance with different people, one on one. We formed a circle around them, gazing upon these dances of beauty. Joshua was very good at dancing. His partners would change frequently, but only because after ten seconds or so the one that was dancing with him would fall apart from the emotion of being close to him. They would crumple to the floor or just simply faint. Then, possessed by what I assumed was The Matchmaker, another person would fling themselves towards him in hopes of a go, and he would calmly and even reverently take the hand of the next person, always asking, "May I have this dance?" as though he was addressing a king or queen. The exaltation he gave others was remarkable.

The dancing was so much fun that I lost track of time, and soon it was late in the day. We had danced all day, and nobody was tired.

And as if they all knew something that I was unaware of, the dancing suddenly stopped and every eye was on the sky as Joshua climbed back up on the stage.

He raised his hands into the air and began to make long waving motions with his arms and hands. As he did, the crowd made sounds of awe and wonder. It took me a second to understand what was happening, but it slowly dawned on me. With every sweeping movement Joshua made with his hands, the sky in the west was being changed. He was moving clouds with his hands, or creating them, I couldn't tell which.

Then came the colors. As though he had an unseen paintbrush in his hand that applied to only the skies, he started to bring magnificent shades of red and orange to the canvas that hung above our heads. He looked like he was writing cursive in the air on an unseen chalkboard, yet with every swoop and flick of the wrist there was a dramatic change in the scenery that mirrored his movements.

Soon, this painted sunset was nothing short of a work of art. There were tints of purple and magenta, even an explosion of green at one point that quickly faded away. It looked like someone had filled a garden hose with every shade of color then soaked the underside of the clouds that hung above. The crowd's stare was glued on Joshua and the sky, watching this display of heavenly fireworks.

Joshua was now slowing his movements, every so often standing back, I assumed in order to observe to see if he felt that his work was satisfactory. He seemed to be nearly finished with his masterpiece. Then, in a last sudden jolt, he flung both his hands towards the horizon. His palms were open and facing away from him, towards the sky. This quick lurch made me think of how one whips their hands when they have gotten something liquid on them that they don't want there, but don't have anything nearby to wipe them off on. When Joshua did this, the sky was splattered with dark, crimson spots that stretched from the northernmost side of the horizon, to the southernmost. It was his finishing touch, and he stood back with a pleased look on his face. He stopped painting, and thus the sky stopped transforming and held its shape as it grew more and more dim.

I thought to myself, "Who is this, that even the sky obeys him with joy?" And just as I was asking myself this question, Joshua looked at me, beaming, and said, "Do your Seers do that?"

It was a playful jab; not intended to harm, but carried just enough of a sting to get my attention and force me to face the honest truth of "no", which I thought, but didn't say. Instead, all I could do was smile.

Sixteen

*E*veryone in the field stayed quiet until the last shred of the sunset disappeared, transforming the sky into a new canvas of black, dotted with the lights of stars that were beginning to come out of their hiding places that they stayed in during the day.

I thought the show was over, but the crowd hadn't stopped watching the sky. Many were now laying down on their backs in the grass, using each other as headrests as they looked upwards.

Joshua began to wave his hands like the conductor of an orchestra, and the crowd began to quietly sing in rhythm with his movements. Their words were simple, repeating over and over, "We love you Father".

Joshua sang with them, and once the entire mass of people, children to elderly, were in rhythm with one another, Joshua's hands began to conduct a new symphony. He had been watching the people, but now he looked to the stars.

In perfect time with the lyrics being sung, Joshua would point at a specific star in the distance. As he did, it would let out a distinct ring, sounding much like a chime, but much more entrancing and beautiful. Every star had a different tone, and he began to accompany the voices with the calm exclamation of the stars. He started slow, a ring here and there, but soon his hands were moving quickly, blazing about, pointing here and there. He became a rush of arms, moving so quickly that one had a hard time in the dim light of the moon to see exactly how fast he was moving. A few times I saw him quickly turn around to point at a grouping of stars behind him, then he spun the rest of the way around, completing the full circle. A song of its own was now being produced, like backup vocals to our leads.

The only way I know how to explain what I saw Joshua do next is just to say it, though I am aware of how odd it sounds. He began to *play* the stars. Instead of briefly pointing at a star like he had been doing, he would hold his point at the star. As long as he did, it would sing an unceasing note. Then, by the same magic, he began to *bend* the note that the star was singing by raising or lowering his pointed finger, the way Pherekydes of Patrae led his orchestra with that first conductor baton. The star would bellow low or belt out a pinnacle note dependent on how low or high he held his outstretched finger, and once in a while in order to bring a crescendo into a portion of the song, Joshua would point at a star, then quickly pull his hand away from it, pulling it across the sky with its tail trailing far behind it until it disappeared. As it shot across the black background it would let out an explosive sound, as though it was a bullet being fired from gun. My mouth was gaping from what I was beholding.

And in the same way that the stars had begun to accompany our voices, the voices now accompanied creation, for the stars were far louder than we were. It was at this point that I noticed that Joshua was still, no longer whirling about. The stars had been jump started, brought to life, and now they went about doing what seemed more natural to them than to hang in the sky and give light. They now seemed to be doing what they were always supposed to do.

Joshua had his eyes closed, almost bathing in the song. It reminded me of the way one cocks their head back in the shower to let the hot water flow over their face and head, receiving of the freshness and heat. He acted like the stars were his own to enjoy, as though they were only designed for the purpose of giving to him. I stood watching him for quite some time, pondering him and these night idolizers of the sky.

We did our best to support the song they sung, but the song they sung had notes in it that we hadn't heard before, thus we were very little help. It wasn't just that they sang notes lower than we had known or notes higher than we had heard (somehow without being shrill to our ears), but new notes altogether, like they found notes in between the notes that were familiar to us. Their repertoire consisted of a gamut none of us could compete with. We faded out unintentionally, the sky took lead, and most began to hum in harmony with the song the singing lights sung.

In the light from the moon, I saw something sparkle on Joshua's face. I realized he was crying, and walked over to the base of the stage to ask him if he was ok.

He nodded and said, "Soon the day will come when what was made will act with the life we once instilled."

I was too tired to ask him what that meant, but I could tell from his response that his tears were not ones of sadness, but joy. It was a broken joy, but joy nonetheless.

Finally, after an extremely long day, it looked as though our time was drawing to a close. The song was dying out above, people's humming had ceased, and some had already begun to stand and slowly made their way off the field towards home.

Joshua came up to Echelon and I, hugged us both, and said, "I hope you enjoyed your time here tonight."

"We did, thank you." I said.

"Good! Would you like more?"

I only had to think about it for a second. What I had beheld tonight seemed completely full of beauty...and honoring to the Eternal.

"Yes." I answered.

"Then, here." Joshua said, as he lightly touched us on our chests with his hand.

Suddenly, everything went black. The only way I know how to describe it is that I felt like I was falling, though not falling as one does in their dreams, awaking in a fright right before they hit the ground. No, this falling was serene, like I was falling, or flying, or quickly sinking, into raw bliss.

My memory of the following moments are sketchy at best. My vision, or memory (I do not know which), would go in and out, come and go, the way your eyes catch a brief picture of what is going on around you in a dark room when the flash from someone's camera goes off. During one of these moments of clarity, I remember loud laughter coming from Echelon and myself. During another I had the distinct impression that we were rolling around on the ground. Lastly, I remember someone passing by saying something to the effect of, "It is like the upper room all over again" in hearty laughter.

I suppose after that, the blackness took the last of my consciousness, for I don't remember anything else from that night.

Seventeen

I woke up in bed at Joshua's house. The last thing I could remember was being at Joshua's feet, and I had no idea how I had gotten from the field, through town and the moving garden, all the way back to the house. I found out later that human bodies can only take so much of Heaven, of "The Matchmaker" as Joshua called him, and past that point they simply shut down. Not to death mind you (the mystics of old tried convincing us of that), but into a place of such peace and rest that consciousness ceases. I had passed out, and was later told that Joshua had carried me from the field back to his house. I was humbled.

I awoke feeling extremely rested, with a clarity of mind that felt as though it could cut diamonds with its sharpness.

I walked outside and made my way through the garden, the plants now larger than I remembered. Maybe they had grown in a very short time, or maybe I was simply taking better notice of them now.

"Hello Scythe!" The familiar voice was becoming more and more pleasant.

"Hello Joshua. How did you sleep?"

"Very well. You?"

"Like I was in heaven."

"Ha! Excellent. Isn't the garden beautiful in the morning?"

"Yes, I was just thinking about that. It seems as though the plants are larger than they were a few days ago."

"Ah, you noticed. Yes, this garden grows very quickly because it is in an atmosphere of life. There is no death or decay to slow it."

I looked down and noticed something that was very odd. There was an orchid at my feet, and as orchids are, beautiful, but this particular orchid had something peculiar hanging off of its stem, below one of the main flowers. It was small, about the size of a coffee bean (I had seen coffee beans back in the days of my enlistment with the Unenlighted, but regrettably, hadn't found any since I joined the Chosen), but more circular, and dark purple. I pointed at it and said,

"What on earth is that?"

"Have you never seen one? Well, I suppose you wouldn't have if you have only witnessed first stage plants. Try it."

"You mean, eat it?"

"Yes. You will be most delighted."

I picked it, smelled it briefly (it had no smell), and popped it into my mouth. If you have ever had a food that was rich but didn't sit heavy in the stomach, then you know what this was like. There wasn't one corner of my mouth that wasn't invaded by a wave of flavor, flavor that can't be adequately put into words, not just because our semantic descriptions fall short, but because the various levels of tastes, flavor upon flavor, were innumerable. But even more impressive was that my stomach was suddenly full. I hadn't eaten breakfast, and now didn't feel the need for it.

"That will give you enough energy and nutrition to last the day. Wonderful, isn't it?" Joshua said.

"It is fantastic!"

I looked down and saw that the orchid from which I had just stolen its berry was producing another in its place, already half ripe.

"You mentioned something about plant stages a moment ago" I said. "What did you mean by that?"

"As I said, this garden isn't under the curse that holds the rest of creation. It is in not limited because the reality of the curse cannot exist where I am. And since I walk through this garden everyday, life is not cut short here. The result is that this garden accesses more of its innate potential that was inbuilt into it at the beginning of time.

All growing things have stages or levels of growth, and many times each stage drastically shifts the nature of the plant or tree from what it was in a previous stage. Sometimes the appearance of a thing in a latter stage is so dissimilar from a former stage that it could be mistaken to be a whole different creation altogether. The plants that you have grown accustomed to are the same plants that grow here, but you have only ever known them in their first stages. In the same way you understand that a sprout is the first stage of a bean plant, here the first stage of an orchid is a beautiful flower. But to stop its life there would be contradictory to how my Kingdom functions. Growth and life never end where I am. Thus, you tasted of the second stage of an orchid. And there are many more stages after that, as is true with anything that grows. Men have a hard time quantifying this concept, and in desperate attempt to make heads or tails of it after witnessing its effect over the expanse of thousands of years, they have credited this facet of creation to evolutionary ideas. But as you can see, it is much more beautiful than that. Come, I will show and explain more."

I followed Joshua about fifty yards down the path (the vines between the cobblestone path still reaching for his heels), towards two very large trees, one I recognized to be a pine. Joshua pointed at the pine and said, "This one is in its first stage and this one" while pointing to the other, "is in a later stage, but both are pine trees."

The second tree he pointed to was, top to bottom, covered by blossoms that were no bigger than an ant, each growing out of the tip of one of the many pine needles. Since there where thousands and thousands of needles, the tree was dressed in a magnificent color of light blue, like it was trying to camouflage itself with the sky. What was even more wonderful was that the tree was losing blossoms every few seconds, so the air swirled with these fragrant flowers, spinning and dancing around us before touching to the ground. None of the flowers on the ground were wilted, and it seemed that they would never wilt for they clothed the ground thickly like snow does, and such a number of flowers meant many of them had fallen long ago, but none where showing their age.

"This only happens in this garden?" I asked.

"No, my friend. There are many places where things grow like this, just not places you have been. Soon though, very soon, all places will grow like this."

Echelon walked up, and Joshua met him a few feet away with a warm embrace.

"Last night was amazing." Echelon said.

"Thank you. I am very glad you enjoyed it. Come, let's sit."

The three of us sat down on the thick cushion of flowers, and Joshua continued.

"I thought this setting would be more suitable for our time together. You both seem to have loosened up a bit, so the office doesn't fit anymore. I found you both today to let you know that this will be our last conversation together."

My stomach dropped. "What do you mean?" Echelon exclaimed, clearly disappointed.

Joshua smiled. "You misunderstand me. You will still be with me, but today is our last conversation where the three of us will talk *together*. From this time forward, we will meet one on one. How does that suit you?"

"Very well." Echelon said.

I wasn't sure how I felt about it honestly. Having Echelon with me when we had our talks with Joshua gave me comfort because I wasn't facing Joshua alone. It wasn't that Joshua was scary or intimidating but that he wasn't intimidated, which resulted in me feeling somewhat unsettled. Most of the tools I had in my bag didn't work on him, and facing him alone gave me the feeling of being cornered, though he was exceedingly unforceful.

"And Scythe, how does it suite you?"

I lied. "It sounds fine."

Joshua raised his eyebrows for a moment, then shrugged and said, "Ok, then that settles it."

"May I ask why you decided to do this?" I said.

"Because we all grow at a different pace. Our hearts either excel us forward at an alarming rate of speed, or they slow us down like an anchor stuck in the mud being drug along by a boat. You are both making steps closer to your destiny, but at different rates. And while it is good to grow with one another, I am not an advocate of slowing one's growth because another doesn't want to move as fast. Thus, we will be meeting separately."

Part of me felt as though I was being left behind, like I didn't have Echelon to lean upon anymore. Oddly enough, I didn't realize until that moment how much of a strength he had been to me, even in his silence. There was something about him, a compass for truth perhaps, that I trusted deep down, though I may reject it at first. He was always running ahead to the place where I would inevitably find myself later.

"And that leads me to the next matter." Joshua turned to Echelon. "I have something I want to talk to you about. I have had you call me Joshua because I was with you that day in the woods many years ago. In fact, that day I taught you about the greatest act of love ever witnessed by humanity."

"What do you mean you were there? Nobody was there. We were alone! Abandoned!" Echelon said, suddenly upset. It was the first time I witnessed Echelon express any kind of anger since he had been changed when we had ridden in his truck together.

"*That* is what I wanted to talk to you about; the anger you feel from the belief that I wasn't with you that day. We need to change that belief so that the anger and offense that is buried deep down in your heart can fade away."

I was totally confused. "I know I am the third wheel in this conversation, but could somebody explain what you two are talking about?"

The were both staring intently at each other, Joshua kindly, Echelon with fire in his eyes and trying to control himself. Whatever Joshua had touched upon was obviously a very tender issue for Echelon.

Echelon turned towards me and explained.

"A very long time ago, when I was only eight years old, I had a friend named Joshua. We were with each other at all times. We slept in the same room, played together all day in the woods, ate from the same plate, and would have left our families for each other. To say that we were best friends would be an understatement; we were one. I can't describe the connection I had with Joshua, even at such young an age. I remember that there was nothing I could say that would cause misunderstanding between us. Everything either of us said was understood in fullness by the other. Such a relationship is not just uncommon, but almost impossible. Nonetheless, we had it."

"It sounds magnificent." I said.

"It was. But short-lived. One day while we were playing in the woods, some of the Chosen bolted through the trees yelling our names. We didn't know why they seemed so angry with us, or why they were running at us with clubs. Naturally when we saw their intensity, instinct was to run. I remember the wood that we were in was the sort that grew close together, thick. This made the chase hard on those behind us because our little bodies could slip through small spaces between brush and small trees, when they had to hack through it to fit. But slowly they gained on us. I was terrified."

"Why were they chasing you?" I asked.

"I'll get to that. Like I said, I didn't know at the time. Anyways, they were gaining on us when Joshua grabbed me by both of my shoulders and abruptly stopped us behind a large stump. I started asking him what he was doing, and told him to run, but he covered my mouth with his hand to silence me, kissed me on the cheek, then shoved me into a fold of the stump. I fell with my back hitting against the bark, and the nearby brush covered me up enough for me to understand that he wanted me to hide. Then he walked out in plain view of the assailants, and ran hard in the direction opposite of me. Every person chasing us followed him, away from me. I wanted to scream out for him to let me come with him, even if that meant that we were slain together, but my mouth was frozen in terror."

Echelon began to cry, then weep, like he had before in the office. Waves of grief and sobbing convulsed through his body, but he continued.

"A few minutes later I heard sounds that I haven't been able to erase from my mind since I heard it. They had caught him, and the thirst they had for blood was being quenched. I stayed glued in one spot next to the stump in disbelief. I couldn't believe it was happening."

He couldn't go on anymore, and really feel apart. I now understood. And somehow, the Joshua we stood with right now knew this story. He looked up at me and finished it.

"Echelon and Joshua's families had been accused of informing the Unenlightened of where the meeting places had been of the Chosen. They killed the entirety of both families."

"I was only spared because of Joshua's sacrifice!" Echelon wailed.

"And is this why you joined the Unenlightened?" Joshua asked.

"Yes."

"It is very understandable."

Echelon suddenly shifted from grief to anger.

"I wanted the Chosen to pay. They had taken everything from me. I hated, and hate, their hypocrisy. They claimed that their god commanded them to not kill long ago, then in the same breath they would quote scriptures where He would kill others Himself. And because they served a hypocritical god, they became hypocrites as well, killing when the cause was great enough or if they believed it was His will. They are totally unpredictable."

Joshua sat quiet, not affirming or denying Echelon's claims.

"This is one reason I like you, Joshua. You say that He does not take life, and nor will you. But you were not there with me that day. We were alone."

"Oh my friend, I was there that day. Tell me the truth, though it is hard; do you feel the same with me as you did your beloved friend of childhood?"

"Yes. It is hard to admit, because it feels like that dishonor's little Joshua, or somehow lessens the connection we had because it used to be something exclusively ours. But it is true; you make me feel as though I can say anything and you will understand the beauty of my heart in it. I feel as though I want to do everything with you and never leave your side. You feel like a grown version of Joshua."

"I am."

"What?" Echelon's eyes squinted and brows pulled in, showing his disapproval and perplexity.

"I am."

Echelon looked intently at Joshua for a few seconds, and Joshua held his gaze with a look that communicated assurance and earnestness. And then almost without knowing why he did, Echelon dove headstrong onto Joshua in an embrace. As he did, inaudible sounds flowed from his mouth, sounding both joyful and mournful, like years of both were finally being released. Joshua held him tight, and they stayed like that for hours. I just watched, not sure as to how all of this made sense. As if Joshua knew my thoughts, he said,

"I came to him as a child."

"Then how are you here now after that child was killed?" I asked.

"It was not the end for me. I am alive and well, as you can see. He needed to learn of what I did for him long ago, and the best way for him to learn it was through him actually experiencing it. Nobody understands grace and love as he does. He has learned it in the most traumatic and real way possible, and it will never leave his heart. This is why he grows so fast; the realities I speak of were planted in his heart long ago."

"I think I understand what you are saying, though you haven't really said it yet." I said. "There was One that came long ago with a story similar to the story you just told. But you cannot be He."

Joshua smiled. "Why not?"

"For many reasons."

"Well, Echelon is convinced. And this is why we must meet one on one from here on out. You have many new questions, questions that I love to be asked, and they will all be answered. But for Echelon to wade through your questions wouldn't be profitable, nor fair, to him. He isn't asking anymore, but enjoying. Like the plants, he has come to a new stage of growth. Come, let's go to my office while Echelon rests."

And with that, we walked Echelon to Joshua's house. Echelon gave his farewell to Joshua by kissing him on the cheek with great reverence and affection, then Joshua and I walked down the path towards the office.

Eighteen

*J*oshua sat across from me in his office, calmly waiting for the questions that he knew I had. I have to admit that at this point I wasn't asking questions so much for the purpose of finding his error so that I felt justified in judging him with guilt, but because I really wanted to know answers. The difference is vast, though they look the same when witnessed. One is motivated by self-righteousness, the other with hunger.

I was the first to speak.

"I guess I could start with your supposed entry. It is tradition to pass down the story through the generations of how He would come. Clouds would be his chariot over the nations, and every eye would see. And this is only one of the many signs that will accompany He who is not false. In order for any of us, and myself, to fully believe, this condition must be met. Sir, have you met this requirement?"

"What does your heart tell you?"

"Joshua, I am not sure what that has anything to do with anything at this point."

"Nonetheless, try to answer the question."

"My heart tells me that you would not lie to me."

"Good. Start at that place firstly. It is always better to start with what you know rather than what you think you know."

He paused for a few seconds. "Now, with your heart

in line, lets confront the mind. Yes, I have met this condition."

"But it says that every eye will see Him! I never saw such a thing."

"That is not true. I saw you, how could you have not seen me?"

"Whatever are you talking about?"

"I did as you have spoken. But there is a reality that you aren't aware of, a reality whose grip is slipping on your mind, but is nonetheless very real. I will explain. Have you ever witnessed someone healed of a phenomenally atrocious disease or deformity, it striking you with joy, but oddly, it not exciting the man next to you that witnessed the same miracle?"

"Yes, many times. They act like you just gave them the news that it may rain in a week rather than that they just witnessed a supernatural wonder. They shrug instead of dance, not so much opposed to what happened, but indifferent."

"Exactly. That is what unbelief can look like in its more understated forms. Have you ever talked to that person a few days, even hours later after the miracle took place, about the miracle?"

I thought for a minute or so. "Yes, I do remember a few times when I did."

"And what was their response?"

"They didn't have one. They had no memory of what had happened."

"Precisely! To not believe results in what we witness to be diminished to nothingness. The minds of men record events in the memory most accurately when an event gives some kind of impression that sticks with them. Otherwise it is usually forgotten. Smallness is rarely noted in the mind, and if what you witness is deemed as small because unbelief has twisted your understanding of events, then you will forget it. Some speak of never witnessing a miracle, but this is impossible. All have witnessed miracles, but some have forgotten because they didn't sufficiently credit what happened to be miraculous in the first place. And that is just the start. Unbelief also causes what we were convinced of to be miraculous in the past to dissipate and disappear into forgetfulness if it is not guarded against with a continual lifestyle of belief. Someone can witness the hand of the Divine in overt workings, be impressed by it, and yet one year later cannot recall the exact story of what happened. The only way to stay convinced of how beautiful something miraculous was, and thusly not to forget it, is to continually remind yourself of it, to relive it again and again in your memory, to write it down, to speak of it to others."

"I understand. This is very true, not only in the lives of those I have been around, but in my own life."

"It is true for all of us. And this is why you don't remember that momentous day."

Suddenly I remembered a conversation I had with a friend of mine, Rachel, during one of our gatherings in the past. It was like some memory bank that I had buried deep within me was instantaneously accessed, and I looked upon the past in my mind with such lucidity that it was as though I was there rather than remembering it.

We were in a undisclosed location in the woods as usual. She asked me if I had seen the newest trickery that the False had implied to deceive the masses. I answered yes rather hastily, then said, "You say he hasn't spilled blood? Any ruler that does not want to rid the world of evil is not worthy of my dedication." We then talked about the technology they had now, the special effects they could implicate, and the money they had to pull it off. Then we went back to our dancing.

"Oh god. That was you?"

"Yes. You were so caught up in what you thought was correct, in your agenda, that you did not welcome me when I came."

My mind wanted to fight his words, to throw another argument at him that would defend what I thought I knew. But I had to be honest; there was no longer much reason to not believe him. It would be a masquerade stemming out of my inability to admit that I was wrong if I acted otherwise. He had nothing to gain from my believing him, and nothing to lose if I didn't. In reality there was nothing in it for him, which made the genuineness of his claims all the more believable.

Plus, I had just seen why I hadn't welcomed him, and my times with him had convinced me that he wasn't who the Seers told me he was. I wasn't sure of everything pertaining to who he was, but I knew from what was spouting up from my heart that my spirit recognized what he said to be true. Though I didn't know everything about him, I was sure of this; he was safe. The implication, I assumed, was that he wouldn't lie to me or exaggerate the truth.

I would have expected to feel joy at this point, but I did not. Instead, I felt an overwhelming amount of regret. Maybe it was because I had pushed so hard against him, even dishonored him, but I suspect the real reason I was feeling regret is because my "agenda" had caused me to miss the very thing I was looking for. I was now seeing that the very framework that I was sure fell within the will of The Eternal and kept me in its center was the very thing that led me far away from it. Grief crept over me, reminding me of the way I felt in the past when I found out that one of the Chosen had been executed by the Unenlightened.

"Joshua, I am so sorry." I said as I hung my head and looked away from him with tears in my eyes.

Joshua smiled, "It is fine, my friend. Do not regret. You may feel that it was all in vain, but it was not. You were still looking for me though you weren't always looking in the right place. You aren't the only one that this happened to. Many didn't recognize me, and still do not."

"But why? How does this happen so easily?" I asked.

"For the same reason it happened to you; because I have come to gather, not to destroy. And that isn't what most people have anticipated of me."

"You have come to gather who?"

"Anyone and everyone that wants to be with me."

"And will you send the remainder left over to go to hell?"

"Never!" Joshua roared. It was the only time I saw him get angry. And I must clarify that I knew He wasn't mad at me, but at such an idea. I think that if I hadn't spent time with him, not having a bit of a grasp of his character like I did now, I would have been sure he was mad at me. It is easy to take someone's words and impart our own wounds into them so that the words turn around and harm us, though they were never aimed at us in the first place. His voice lowered, but it was still intense.

"I desire that none would perish. I have never, and will never, send any person to that place. It was never created for them to begin with. And though I do not send anyone there, some insist on choosing to go there anyways. "

"How so?"

"Choice is a reality in every realm, even when one is in the Place of everlasting bliss. They choose. And I don't say "choose" in a sense that implies that they made an uninformed decision, like the Eternal is trying to trap people there. He would never do such a thing, and has spent thousands of years working for the sole purpose of trying to get people not to go there. They actually *choose* to go there, all the while well informed with what they are doing. Those who seek find. Those who knock it is opened."

"But that is an awful place. Why would they do that?"

"Lewis captured as to why in *The Great Divorce*. Have you read it?"

"Why, yes! My grandpa gave me an old tattered copy. Marvelous work."

"That is why they go. Men's minds become so distorted that the place that lies below becomes more like home than where I want them to live. Where we are is too clean, too bright, too solid and real. They are like eyes that have adjusted to a dark room and how uncomfortable it is when someone suddenly flips on the light. Anytime they see any fragment or residue of our land they *beg and beg* for it to be taken away from them. Like I said, it is their choice, so we do as they ask. Thankfully, my life and redemptive power reaches further than you know. My love has no limits. David said that even if he made his bed in Sheol he would find me there, or rather, that I would find him. People cannot hide from my love but they can choose not to receive it. You must understand; I don't like them being there. This is one reason why I sign the sky on regular occasion, insinuating to the Great Sacrifice. I want them to be constantly reminded that it is always available, and always free. All one must do is come to me and receive a *free gift*. If that is too hard for someone to do, well, then I am sorry. One can't make something more easy to receive than to make it free."

"It is incredibly sad that a person would choose not to accept a free gift, especially when its rejection has such large implications."

"Yes it is. It weighs very heavy on my heart. It is not only the ones that choose to be there that suffer, but the rest of us suffer as a direct consequence to their decision as well!"

"I suppose that it is true, though it has never occurred to me before. Its not like those that have gone ahead are forgotten about, or that anyone loves them any less when they leave, despite how lost and broken they were when they died."

"Exactly."

"You said that you have come not to destroy, but to gather. That is very different from what I have been taught. Can you explain?"

"Of course. It is very simple actually. If there is one thing you take away from our times together, I hope it will be what I am about to tell you. Long ago I told my followers, as well as the writers that wrote the ancient holy writings, that I would come again. I told them that many would come in my name, preaching a gospel that differed from the one that I preached the first time I walked the earth, and in turn, that my followers needed to reject their message as false. Scythe, do you know what my message was, and still is?"

"Love?"

"That is correct. Love is so core to who I am that it could even be my name. My message was many things, but boiled down to a few words and more poignantly put, it was to love, especially to love our enemies. That was a radical concept in that day. Seems it still is. Sadly, the very characteristic that those who profess to know me are looking for in a messiah is to destroy their enemies. It was the same then. They were waiting for a king that would come and bring them justice, which is not a bad desire. But the way they envisioned this taking place was wholly incorrect. They pictured their king bringing justice the only way they knew how; by force. I did not do this for them. The only force I used was to heal the sick, raise the dead, and forgive the unforgivable. I chose to be killed rather than kill.

Honestly, I wasn't what they wanted. And I still am not. I haven't changed. I have come with the same gospel that I preached then. I have come in peace. I have come not to condemn, but to love. I have come to give life, not to take it. I have not come to bring destruction or punishment, but to gather those that desire to be with me. My Father and I have no reason to punish or destroy people. I have not come for the purpose of sin, for sin was defeated long ago."

"No wonder they killed you. This is a wonderful message, but one that isn't easily swallowed."

Joshua laughed. "Only for those stuck in the old ways of thinking. Lance, Natalia, and Richard never choke on their daily bread. They truly think that the good news is good. I'm not sure how being a guy that doesn't want to kill others is a bad thing, but no matter. Man assumes that I am as uncreative and limited as they are with how to deal with problems, but I am not. The repertoire of man pertaining to ways to deal with problems is in short supply, with the last step being 'ah, just be rid of it.' But I can redeem anything."

"That is beautiful, but what about what it says of you in the last book of the ancient scriptures? You are saying the very opposite of what it seems to portray of you at points."

"Yes, it seems to speak of much destruction coming from my hands. But the only thing that ever came from my hands was my own blood. Remember, scripture records that I don't even take the life of my greatest enemy. That should speak volumes.

More accurately, the judgments you have read about in that book, and what one can witness afflicting the Unenlightened even today, are not the manifest justice of The Eternal working on the behalf of the Chosen, or even the Embrace for that matter. At first glance that would seem to be true, but only if one believes that the Eternal only loves a portion of his children rather than all of them. He loves all, but some choose to live in a way that gives darkness the legal right to afflict them. And *that* is the key.

At least when pertaining to the supernatural afflictions on the earth, it isn't so much divine protection that the Chosen and the Embrace experience as much as it is that they are never the intended party for these judgments to begin with. They are judgments, don't mistake that, just not judgments coming from the Eternal. The source from where calamity comes from has always been the question of the ages. I am the revealing of the answer.

The reason the Unenlightened are afflicted by the horrors hovering over the earth is not because they are fighting against the Chosen or even because they are evil, but because they allow darkness to afflict them by agreeing with it through sin. Even in this hour, darkness cannot afflict those on earth unless it gains the agreement of those originally entrusted with dominance over the earth. And in these days, agreement of that sort is easy to find because the Unenlightened so regularly engage in activities that open wide the doors of their lives to allow darkness to do whatever it pleases to them. All of this isn't so much about justice, wrath, or the destruction of evil, but evil having the right to war upon itself. Wrath is solely in the hands of darkness, never The Eternal. Only love is wielded by The Eternal. He has no reason to destroy evil; It is doing that all by itself!"

Joshua chuckled under his breath as he paused, like he was reflecting upon what he had just said, then continued.

"Don't get me wrong; divine protection is in play during these days. The Chosen are protected for two reasons; because they have let the Great Sacrifice drip over them, and because they do their best at abstaining from activities that gave darkness a legal right to harm them. When the Unenlightened come to harm the Chosen or the Embrace, and thusly exert the power of their own will, the Eternal steps in with his unseen peacemakers, not to harm anyone or to wipe the Unenlightened off the face of the earth, but simply to foil their plans. He is so creative that His ways are many in doing this."

This was all a bit much for my mind to compute. "Are you saying that we should just rip that book out of the ancient scriptures? Isn't it inspired like the rest of it?"

"Of course it is inspired. And no, I am not suggesting that one be rid of that book. Anything inspired offers much to gain from. Rather I would explain it like this; I said that if anyone came preaching a gospel about me that differed from the one I gave to you when I was on earth, it should be considered lacking truth. The good news is that I am good. And that last book is blessed, but it does portray a view of me that is drastically different from the picture painted of me when I was on the earth, doesn't it?"

"I suppose so."

"In fact, one could say that the core values that I communicated while on earth were completely excluded from that last, blessed book. One could easily make an argument that how I was portrayed in that apocalyptic vision gives rise to a completely different gospel.

I am not suggesting that you disregard that book, but that you hold higher the truth demonstrated of who I am in my first visit to earth. Derive my character first and foremost from my own words and actions rather than the words and actions of those following me.

You must remember that the fact that I am holistically good, with no fraction of darkness in me, was quite a new idea when I came the first time, and it called for a significant mental shift in the minds and hearts of the religious population of that day, the writer of that vision included.

Think of how they thought of me before I came; I was credited with taking men's lives over the smallest of issues, a bi-polar maniac, ready to fly off the handle over the most minute infraction. I was dressed up by the fears and imaginations of men, totally disguising who I really am. Thus, I came and walked the earth to bring clarity to my nature. I did not destroy sinners but loved them and invited them into my embrace. And I have not changed since then. I am good.

I know exactly what the Chosen, and the Seers at that, want of me in order that they ascribe to believing that I am the messiah. They are looking for a violent judge of the nations that will bring what they call justice. I will bring justice, but I refuse to do so in the way they want. I will only do it through love, through forgiveness, through healing, through redemption. It's as if they have forgotten that isn't exactly what they experienced that initially drew them out of their depravity! What if I had dealt with them in the way that they want me to treat their enemies!"

Though I had drank my fill of Grace time and time again, I couldn't deny that I had hypocritical places in my heart that wanted others to pay for what they did. I watched babies be killed, and if I am totally honest, the only fit payment in my mind for the actions of those that instigated such an atrocity was death. In fact, on that note, if I traveled far enough into the dark recesses of my heart, I could have easily found places in me that would feel that torture preceding death would be *more* just than just ending their life. Joshua didn't seem to hate such an act any less than I, but he did deal with it differently. He confounded my thinking; thinking that was now becoming more and more limited and carnal to me.

"I really like what you are saying, Joshua. I want to believe it. But I am still stuck on the issue of what the scriptures say of the messiah near the end of time. You do not fit the mold."

"I understand that. You have been taught one way for quite some time; it is hard to suddenly shift everything in a matter of minutes. Do you remember when you and I talked about a source of revelation that was greater than the scriptures?"

"Yes."

"You told me if such a thing did exist, then you would look to that source of revelation for guidance. Do you remember saying that?"

"Yes."

"That source of revelation is standing before you. I am the Truth. I am the Way. I am Life. The scriptures merely point to me, and if something I say runs against the grain to what they seem to suggest, be assured that they are what are skewed, not Me."

Though I was convinced Joshua was who he claimed to be, I couldn't help but still have second-thought flashbacks of what the Chosen or the Seers would think or say to what I was being taught. This was the case in this situation; I immediately thought of what the Seers would think of Joshua's last statement. Most assuredly, they would be absolutely infuriated, feeling justified in their judgments, pointing to Joshua's statement as proof that he was one of The False or a cult leader that demanded full submission to his every teaching.

It was odd to be so sure of something now (Joshua), yet still have lingering thoughts that so persistently questioned what I was so sure of. Something loitered around in my heart that was no longer invited to stay. I wondered how it got there in the first place until I realized that there was a time when I once welcomed it to dictate my thoughts and feelings. Now it felt more like a remnant of something left over rather than a driving force, something my heart was gaining the strength to ask to leave. Soon, I hoped, my heart wouldn't be so polite about it and would just force it to leave, threatening it with violence if it did not comply.

Yet I wasn't there yet. And because of this whispering commentary into the ears of my heart whenever Joshua laid down more weighty truths, I sometimes had to take Joshua's words on faith. But maybe what I felt is better described as trust. I was trusting who he was rather than the truth he was teaching me. I could *do* that. This brought me full circle back to the truth in question, with which I was then more able to blindly grasp. I had to do it this way rather than just being able to jump in with all of me. And so was the case in this situation.

"I suppose I have been with you long enough to begin to give myself to that idea."

Joshua could tell by the tone of my voice that my sentence didn't communicate the end of my thought.

"But?" He asked.

"But the problem with what you are presenting lies with the fact that many only know of you *because* of the scriptures. And in one book you are peaceful and loving, and the other you seem to be angry and destructive, pouring out wrath upon the nations and taking *many* lives. How are they supposed to know which person you are? How are they supposed to legitimize just mincing the scriptures up like you are suggesting?"

"Firstly, I don't want it to be minced, but properly ordered. There is a reason why my life on earth was recorded from four different angles giving four congruent views, written by four different men, presented in four different books, yet with one stark conclusion; that I am peaceful, loving, and good. These four books are the closest account to who I am. There wasn't much room for the writers to write into the script their own interpretation of the events. They simply recorded fact: my words and actions. It couldn't be skewed. All the scriptures are true, but some are more true than others. Prioritize the account of my life, my teachings, and my actions firstly and you will steer clear of beliefs that will slow down your growth.

I perfectly represent the Eternal. Every characteristic in His nature is present in me at all times. Thus, you now know who He really is, for you know me. If you have seen my character, you have seen His.

Now, I challenge you with this: You must let the nature of the Eternal determine the ancient writings, not the ancient writings determine the nature of the Eternal. This is quite a switch for most; but an imperative one."

"I will try. But that is the best I can promise for now." It wasn't that I didn't believe him, but that he had unloaded so much on me that I hadn't had a chance to gain my balance quite yet. I had a lot to absorb into my heart and mind that he had just taught me, and probably even more to learn in the coming days.

"And that is all I require; willingness."

"It makes sense, but I am still just taking all of this on blind faith, because I trust you. I don't think it is my own yet. Don't get me wrong; I feel as though I just stumbled upon a treasury or a well kept secret."

"You have, my friend." He smiled. "I feel the same way when I am with you."

"Joshua, but what of your name? How should I refer to you?"

"Joshua will do. It is actually my name. There are other names that are more known that you could call me, but those seem to make spirits manifest, always setting off debate and wasting everyone's time. Lets stick with Joshua."

152 | THE COMING

Nineteen

Our meeting was over. We had wrapped up and walked out of Joshua's office, now heading off to find Echelon.

I was trying to process everything Joshua had just told me. Surely if anything, what he had told me was a new view to consider. But I had learned that writing something off to merely "a new, interesting view" usually indicated that one wasn't going to give themselves over to it, but instead just tolerate it for a time.

I could do the same. I could believe what I always had and build up my doctrines like a barrier around my mind and heart so that nothing I hadn't agreed to had any ability to assault me with its foreignism. I could do that. But Joshua, Joshua himself, not so much the way he explained the world *but his person*, made me relax and not take those things so seriously. I was realizing that what I thought was the safest route in the past was sometimes the most dangerous. Rigidity may have ensured that truth wouldn't be bent, but instead it would suddenly snap altogether, revealing how untrue it was to begin with. It is very easy to put faith into what seems to be real when it is merely a shadow of a greater, better reality.

I wouldn't do the same. Joshua's character, his personality, made me more than consider everything he said. Perhaps it was his laughter alone. And it wasn't like he was trying to win me to his argument (though he wouldn't call our conversations that). He seemed to care less what I believed, like it would all be sorted out in time either way. But I didn't want to wait: I believed his words. Or, I should say that I chose to believe them. There is a difference.

We soon found Echelon resting at the house, reclining on a couch, reading a letter. He hadn't changed his physical appearance in any way, but he looked better somehow, more whole, brighter.

"Hello!" He said happily.

Joshua and I greeted him, and he held the letter above his head, making us take notice of it.

"You know what this is?" Echelon asked.

"No." I said. "Who is it from?"

"From the Seers."

"What does it say?"

Echelon handed the paper to me. "Read it for yourself."

This is what I read:

```
To Whom It May Concern,

    We regret to inform you that the
allotted   time   period   for   your
mission has run its course. We can
only conclude that you have failed
in bringing the heretic in question
to  his  knees  in  surrender.  The
effect  of  your  lack  of  action  is
threefold.
1) You have been relieved of your
responsibilities  to  this  case.  We
believed  we  could  rely  upon  you,
but  we  were  wrong.  You have failed.
A  more  efficient  replacement  has
```

already been sent in your stead:
Joe Tetzel.
2) Expect disciplinary action to be
taken upon your arrival back home.
3) If your arrival is delayed, it
will be assumed that you have taken
sides against the Chosen and the
Counsel of the Seers, and swift
action will be taken to remove any
threat that you pose.

In clemency and truth,
The Seers
[Speaking for the Chosen]

"I didn't even know there *was* a time restraint we were under." Echelon said. Nor did I.

Joshua shook his head. "They can't touch you. Do not be worried."

I wasn't so sure. I knew of many stories of people that the Seers suspected of being turncoats, and they never ended well. Apparently, Echelon was aware of this reality as well, only his experience struck much closer to home than my own.

"Joe Tetzel. Are they kidding?" Echelon said in disbelief.

"I'm afraid not. They still call upon him regularly." I said.

"I thought he had retired." Echelon said.

"Only from fulltime work. He still gets called in for special cases. I guess Joshua qualifies for such a case."

Joe was legendary among both the Chosen *and* the Unenlightened. He was the kind of legend that is spoken of so frequently that there was no way that all the claims about him could be staked by first hand witnesses, thus they were probably rumors, but rumors that he himself never denied or dismissed so over time they transformed back to actuality. I believe he knew this lack of denial would strengthen the effect of his reputation, if in just to cause the hair to stand up on the back of someone's neck when his name was spoken. His reputation was now so well established that the intimidation it caused paved the way before him so that when he arrived he rarely had to resort to his methods any more. He was said to be calm and reserved in nature, but capable of snapping at the most unexpected times in which he would exert the most brutal and instantaneous rage. In these frenzies there were no limits set upon what his hands would do, like his being had been taken over by another. It was said that as quickly as he had lost control over his fury he would regain it again, and this was even more terrifying to people than what he did during these rages. It was just plain eerie. He would pat his hair back down so that it laid flat on his head again, adjust his tie, maybe wipe his hands off if they were now wet, and pick up a conversation like nothing had happened. It was the lack of conscience in it all that was so disconcerting, as well as his unpredictability. When one was with him, so I heard, it felt like you were walking with a grenade that had lost its pin. You were just waiting.

Mr. Tetzel was a middleman. He was made use of in high-tension situations by the Counsel of the Seers when they weren't making headway in a situation and needed more "effective" means from which to derive their desired outcome. When they had washed their hands of a situation, they dirtied his instead of their own. When dealing with a traitor, he was the one to conduct the "interview", though it could hardly be called that. He hadn't failed to get even one of his interviewees to tell him the full truth about what they had done, even if the "truth" was just what he wanted to hear, not what they had done at all. That is how pain works; they will say anything for it to stop. Joe was also quite good at taking offerings from the Chosen, if good means getting every penny from the crowd in ways that are wholly intimidating. It was common knowledge that when he stood upon the stage and spoke of money, people trembled and gave their all.

"I guess we have to decide if we are going to report back to the Seers or not." I said.

Echelon responded. "Are you kidding? I didn't sign up for another organization, but an encounter. And he is standing right next to us. There is no way I am leaving, come hell or high water."

I wasn't as sure. There wasn't a question in whether or not I enjoyed being here; I did. But Echelon hadn't been with the Chosen as long as I had. There was much more for me to leave behind than for him. And though there were apparent problems in the Chosen, there were also many beautiful things that would be cut out of my life.

The Chosen was my spiritual family. I knew hundreds of them on an intimate level, and whether our beliefs differed now or not, I didn't care. I loved them as they were. I knew them and was known by them. To leave all of those relationships didn't seem like the only option.

Plus, I would miss out on the gatherings. They were a different flavor from Joshua's meetings, but I still loved them. Most of all though, if I am honest, was that I was respected and honored in the Chosen. I was recognized as one that had been faithful for many years to the Chosen and the Eternal, and it was a place where I was never assaulted with dishonor. That was comforting for a man.

I felt as though I had been given an ultimatum by the Seers, and I detested them for it, but I knew what I had to do.

"I think I want to go back." I said.

"What?" Echelon shrieked.

"There is too much to leave behind. This can't be the way it was supposed to be. Let me go back and simply set things straight, then I will try to come back here."

Echelon was getting more worked up. "I can't believe this. You have seen the man behind the curtain, and now you want to go try to befriend him? Joshua is all we need!"

"Echelon." Joshua said calmly. "Scythe is free to decide what he wants." He didn't seem surprised, but I couldn't help but notice the faint reminisce of sadness that he was doing his best not to wear on his face.

"I know he is, but he is being a fool. They may kill him for all we know." Echelon said.

Joshua spoke slowly. "Echelon, when someone does something we disagree with we can either call them fools and speak death to the path they have decided to walk, which invites upon them the very thing we are concerned about, or we can bless them irregardless of how we feel about it. If we really want him to be okay, we will bless. Love never looks like control."

"You are right. Scythe, if you are decided about this, then we will do everything and anything we can to assure that it goes smoothly."

"I am decided. I leave tonight."

Twenty

I will spare you the much of the details of my journey back. I walked through the night, sometimes even jogged, knowing that I needed to get back as soon as possible so as to avoid any assumptions made about me.

I will say that as I walked and jogged I came face to face with what I had forgotten was actuality; destruction. Maybe it was the swirl of events that had taken place, or maybe it was the sheer beauty of places like Joshua's garden (perhaps even Joshua Himself), but I had forgotten that most of the world did not look like the town of The Embrace did. Everywhere that Joshua was not was not intact. It had escaped me how bad it was. Landscapes were sometimes completely burned to the ground, huge cracks in the earth's crust could be seen plainly, and rusty metal wreckage from old cars or tanks was everywhere. It wasn't that the earth wasn't still beautiful (one could still find life here and there), but rather, hurt.

This journey gave me ample time to think, which I was thankful for. I was finally alone; nobody's opinions but my own to dwell upon. I felt that for the first time in a long while I had the chance to come to some of my own conclusions about what I had been experiencing for the past few days without there being anybody to influence me but me. I had heard enough from everyone else; it was time to hear from myself.

Oddly, when it was finally time to hear from myself, in many ways I drew a blank. I wasn't totally sure where I was at. It wasn't that I felt confused, but that I felt that maybe I didn't have to choose a side after all; The Embrace or The Chosen. Both sides seemed to have a grasp on things that were true, so I didn't see why I had to come to any sort of conclusion in the first place.

But I supposed that the main deciding factor in it all was how I felt about Joshua. Perhaps that isn't the correct way of phrasing it, because how I *felt* about him was clear now. He was impossible not to like. The real question had more to do with truth, and I knew the Seers would come from this perspective.

I couldn't deny that the logic Joshua set forth, whether it appealed to my heart or to my mind, was very convincing. And I will admit that I felt convinced of his claims, at least mostly convinced. It takes time to relearn what you thought you knew, especially when you have believed something for as long as I had.

I believe the only thing that was keeping that last shred of concern embedded in my heart and mind about Joshua had nothing to do with what he had done or said at all. Instead it was because the very thing I had been warned against had happened; I had listened long enough to be convinced. Thus, I had either been deceived in the exact way I had been warned about, or I had been warned incorrectly. I couldn't help but question both.

Had I been duped, reeled into falsity and deception, which worried me because the judgement for such an error seemed to be quite intense, or had I simply discovered something true and hidden that had not yet been opened up to the Chosen? Had I been wrongly warned from the start or was I just plain gullible, easily susceptible to error? I thought that I was more resistant to foreign ideas than the common man, but maybe I was just as thin-skinned as anyone else.

Some place in me knew that the motive that sat behind the wheel and drove my questioning of if I had been deceived, was fear. I was aware of this on a level that couldn't quite be categorized as total consciousness, but nonetheless recognition, for I could feel my stomach churn when I thought about it. The thought of mistaking blasphemy as truth terrified me. And antithetically, I questioned my past simply because Joshua had painted a whole new picture of The Eternal (and life itself) that seemed much more beautiful than what I had known. This second motivation was more like intrigue, curiosity, and wonder all wrapped up into one feeling. I suppose it felt much like how I would guess one feels when they are given a map leading to some buried fortune by a man breathing his last breath; You can try to deter the person from going on a quest to discover and uncover the riches, but your warning will be in vain. He will go.

Both motivations were impossible to ignore (whether it be fear or intrigue), and equally impossible to come completely conscious of as well. Everything snooped just below the surface.

Like a splinter under the skin too deep to remove because the self inflicted operation may cause too much pain to the one with it embedded, I left my concerns right where they were, hoping that they would take care of themselves with enough time. I didn't have to wait long.

I arrived in town and went to find the gathering for the night. I knew the Seers would be there, and maybe I could straighten this whole thing out with them. I knew of a few places that hadn't been found by the Unenlightened, and banked on the Chosen being at one of those locations. I was fortunate to find the gathering rather quickly, and made my way through the crowd looking for one of the Seers. Immediately I noticed that something was wrong. I passed through the crowd and saw many people that I knew and loved, but none of them acknowledged my presence in the least bit. They weren't being overtly mean, just apathetic and passive to my being there, which hurt just as badly. After a bit it occurred to me that I wasn't just not feeling accepted but one worse; rejected. I couldn't make heads or tails as to why, so I pulled an old friend aside and asked him why it felt as though nobody was excited to see me. It turned out that the Seers had told the people of our delay in converting Joshua, and assumptions had been made by all. They were now treating me as an outsider.

This astounded me. I had known these people for *years*, and in no more than a week's time their opinion of me had changed virtually overnight. What had I actually done wrong that would constitute such judgments to be made towards me? We still served the same Divine Source; how could we be that different? And even if we were different now, were we different enough to legitimize such shunning?

What surprised me the most was that I had been a member of the Chosen longer than most of the people at this gathering, but they had the audacity to deem *me* to be the one lacking wisdom and insight. Maybe that is my pride speaking, but nonetheless it astounded me that my experience weighed so little to them.

My years of faithful service obviously gained me no real credibility either, for what is credibility worth if not tested for its purity in a situation where there was potential for misunderstanding and distrust. If credibility could erode so quickly when I hadn't actually *done* something or confessed to anything, then it wasn't credibility, nor relationship, to begin with. And if one couldn't have their trust after so much time, trust being merely the giving of the benefit of the doubt when everything points to your guilt, then what was the point of being involved in the first place? Suddenly everything I had weaved together for so long was unraveling before my eyes. I felt like a house built on an unseen shifting foundation, it only falling now, after so many years, because the shaking finally came. A need grew up in my heart for something solid to build my life upon, something to give myself to, something that wouldn't yank itself out from underneath me.

It was then that my eyes swept over the crowd of people that were present and I realized something that I had never realized before. The only way to explain it is to say that what had once seemed glorious now seemed less bright. I couldn't make any sense of it. What was once full of liberty to me now seemed boxed-in and generic, even claustrophobic, like a suburban housing development. At first I thought that the meetings had dipped in measure of Heaven's presence since I had been gone, but then it occurred to me that it hadn't changed at all; I had.

It wasn't that what I had called glory before wasn't in fact glorious, but that it was a lesser glory than what Joshua exuded. The brightest glory we had beheld in the Chosen after days and weeks of worship and fasting was muted, possibly even gloomy, in comparison to what Joshua effortlessly emitted at any moment of the day. What had been to me glory that would have caused one to veil their face was now no more to me than the heat that a light bulb gives off. It was nonetheless *light*, but light that seemed dim when compared to Joshua.

I was both excited by this moment of clarity and saddened by it. It made me excited because perhaps my newfound discoveries were not misled, but sad because if they weren't, I had spent a long time settling for less than what I could have had, as was also true of my spiritual family amassed around me.

Then, off in the distance, I saw Rachel. Hope welled up in my heart. Surely, if there was anyone that I trusted and trusted me, it was her. We had watched too many atrocities together to not understand and trust each other. All the times we sang beside each other and sat in the Brilliance together gave us a special confidence in each other.

"Rachel!" I called out joyfully, happy to see her.

"Hello Scythe." She said plainly, without a smile. Her eyes darted back and forth, watching those around us rather than looking at me.

"How are you? It is wonderful to see you."

"I am fine Scythe. I am quite busy at the moment though." She muttered.

"Busy with what?"

"Uh, many things I suppose."

Her discomfort was obvious. "Rachel, don't tell me you believe what they said about me."

"How could I not?" She blurted out. "You were gone too long to not have been affected by the heretic's teachings and words. Nobody has lasted that long around him without being distorted in thought."

I didn't feel distorted in thought, though I was open to correction if I needed it. I didn't want to leave humility behind (as I had seen some do when they had learned something new), and I wanted others to feel free to speak into my life in case I had left the narrow road without knowing it. But now that I was back with the Chosen, I *did* notice that there was something different about me; something happier, clearer, more carefree. I wouldn't have noticed unless I had been back in a familiar setting.

"I don't think I believe anything now that should keep the two of us from having what we did a few of days ago." I said.

"I am not so sure. You were innocent then, free from the teachings he is spreading." She said.

"I am not sure what is so awful about what he is teaching, or what is so threatening about what he does...."

My voice trailed off as soon as it occurred to me how what I was saying would sound to Rachel. I didn't know what she had been told of Joshua, but they were most likely heretical notions, which I had just inadvertently endorsed by saying what I had. Sometimes before you speak you have to hear what someone else will hear in your words, for it could be galaxies from what you are trying to communicate. The best thing to do at that point is to stop talking, which I did.

So is the problem with revelation. One can have an issue quite clearly communicated to them by the Eternal in a way that makes sense, while another can hear about the same issue through the grapevine of men and it be like chalk in their mouth. Likely, the two will never see eye to eye, for each heard a very different thing, though it was the same thing all along. Some matters can only be communicated between The Eternal and man, not man and man, in a way that truly convinces and sticks to the heart and mind. Reaching out and taking hold of revelation, as elusive as it can be to a daft mind, has so much to do with who communicates it.

Rachel paused, and then spoke calmly.

"I know you don't find a problem with what the heretic and false messiah is teaching. But I do. And that makes things different between the two of us. I am sorry Scythe, but I cannot be affiliated with you anymore."

I couldn't believe what I was hearing. It was so sudden and without grief or sadness, the way the blade of Madame Guillotine falls. I got very dizzy in a way that wasn't like what Joshua or the Immersion caused me to experience. The woods spun for a bit, and I had to sit in order not to fall over. I found tears dripping down my face, confused with what I had done.

I was eager to repent of any legitimate sin I was walking in, if someone could only show me in the scriptures where I had gone wrong. But none could. At least nobody could show me any scriptures that weren't far-flung, desperate attempts at plainly condemning Joshua or myself, still without any real reason. The ones they tried to show me were so inapplicable that I almost laughed. It was as though they had started with a conclusion and verdict and were now trying to legitimize them with scripture rather than the other way around.

They would skip over what we had actually done wrong and head straight for the verses that spoke of punishment. I assumed this was because they didn't really know what we had done wrong but still felt that we were wrong, and had to show us the punishment for our actions if we didn't repent. So it is when you make a judgment about someone else. The most "love" you can offer to them is to remind them of the chastisement awaiting them if they don't renounce what they believe. It was an illogical circle of reasoning and the only way out was to agree with them. I *so* desired to be wrong. If only I was, for then I could save and mend what relationships I had before. But even when I looked for it, searched for it, even tried to create it, I couldn't find fault in what I had done or said, which was true of Joshua as well. And most didn't give me a chance to give my side of the story anyways. It was an open and shut case before it ever went to court.

In short, I spoke to the Seers, but they were more cold and unwilling to listen than Rachel had been (Rachel at least let me talk). It was clear that in order to be officially accepted back into the Chosen, I had to renounce Joshua and his teachings. It was an ultimatum; one I learned later that most people are given that go on to make some sort of positive impact upon humanity.

And while the Seers overtly voiced the choice they were setting before me, Joshua was also giving me a decision; a question stated without ever opening his mouth and saying it, nor with any implicative loss attached to it if I made the wrong decision. *Who he was* set forth a question. He was asking me to trust his character before I understood everything.

It would be a lie to say that I wasn't tempted to recant. There was so much that I loved at stake. From one angle it looked worth it. I knew that just as fast as I had lost everything, I could gain it back with a few words. It would be so easy, so comfortable, so simple.

But it also occurred to me that if I recanted I would forever know in my heart that I had compromised.

Something was more true about what I knew now, even if I couldn't put my finger on exactly what yet. And I didn't think I could live with the regret that came from the knowledge of my compromise; the knowledge that maybe there was more and I was on the precipitous of possessing it but didn't jump.

So I leapt. I did not recant. Joshua hadn't done anything that deserved me to desert him like that. It wasn't so much about theology or right beliefs (though it was for them) as much as it was that I now valued Joshua as a friend, and I refused to give up on a relationship as quickly as the Seers and the Chosen apparently did. I didn't want to have the least bit of resemblance to their disloyalty.

Words like "excommunicated" and "handed over to darkness" were said. At this point, they also let me know they had sold my house, telling me that the Eternal owned it anyways. I have to admit that while it hurt violently when they escorted me out of the room and told me to never come back, it also felt very right, like I had just taken my first breath of air. Unseen weights fell off me that had been pulling on me since I arrived, and I felt very free, probably the way a woman feels who finally divorces her abusive husband. The world was open to me in a new way, and I felt as though I could take from it and experience it as I pleased.

It didn't surprise me anymore that the Chosen hadn't recognized Joshua in his coming. He wasn't what they wanted or expected, though he had showed them long ago exactly what he was like.

My resolve was now more concrete, which had been soft when I arrived. What I had secretly suspected was fact; it had been a sham. Not all of it mind you, just the inner workings of it; the cogs and gears. The Chosen did live victoriously in these days. Much should be credited to them for that. They had been fed for years prior to these days of turmoil with the belief that we were going to evade this era completely, or be in the midst of it barely surviving. Yet the Chosen weren't barely surviving; they were thriving. They were exceedingly victorious. To say that they were not would have been a lie. Miraculous provision, protection, and restoration kept us more than intact, and we won more people to our cause than any other time in history. The disasters spoken of by the Seers of old did in fact befall humanity; we just prospered in the midst of it due to The Eternal's workings in our midst.

I now saw how I could have believed both, even just hours ago. Both sides, Joshua and the Chosen, had truth. But now knew that I could not believe both and still be true to both at the same time. One was greater, and to give myself to the lesser truths would be selling myself short. It was like choosing to breath air at sea level or at a great elevation; they both contain air, but one would let me run for miles when the other would only feed my lungs enough to take four or five steps before I was winded. Both were air. One just had more of it.

I now had perspective. What I had previously considered a gift had finally been unwrapped. Now I wanted to put it back under the tree.

I don't believe I would have realized anything was awry pertaining to the Chosen unless I had been rejected firstly. Their subtle rejection caused me to instinctively stand back and evaluate the whole scene. It is odd how things we cower from sometimes work to be our saving grace. Rejection was the last thing I desired to happen to me when I woke up that morning, and yet by nightfall, rejection had been used to help me enter into what I believed was going to be the greatest joy I had experienced up until that point. I felt as though I was lining myself up for the fullness of what The Eternal had for me. This was a very, very good feeling.

I knew where I wanted to go. I knew what, or rather who, I wanted the house of my life to rest upon. This time it would be a person rather than an organization; relationship instead of religion.

Every step I took away from the town I had lived I felt both joy and pain increase. Joy because I knew where the road I walked on was headed; a new, more wonderful home. And pain because I left family behind, but family that didn't consider to be related to me anymore. I wondered if family is still family if it rejects you and throws you to the streets. Oddly enough, they thought that was the most loving thing to do towards me. They actually told me that with tears in their eyes. It was all very strange and contradictory.

Something told me that the pain would wane after time, and that many of those I left behind would find the same path I had, and make the journey to the same Lowly Splendor that I had found, or more accurately, been helped to find. Maybe then we would be family again, rejoined over Who we loved rather than what we believed.

Twenty-One

I was miles from the town of the Embrace when I saw him. He was far away, running towards me on the road, dust swirling up behind him, and as always, a smile beaming from his face.

At that moment, the last of something that I had tried to be rid of for years suddenly died and a thing much more childlike took its place. I found myself sprinting as well, and neither one of us thought to slow down when we got close.

His arms caught me as we came together, our collision not harming either of us. I felt the strength of grip around my sides and breathed in deeply of his masculine scent. This comforted me. He spoke; his voice was even more gentle than normal.

"Family can mean many things, my friend. I am so sorry they do not understand you. If it helps, the issue doesn't lie with you, but with you knowing me. Maybe that will make it feel a bit less personal."

I'm not sure why, maybe because I felt safe, but something of hurt deep inside me that I didn't know was there started to bubble up. Grief of such degree that I did not know existed came up and spread over the whole of me. I was crying and crying, now very aware of what I had been trying to shut out; what I had just left behind. But it was not just that; it was everything that had ever happened. I remembered deaths, betrayals, stumblings, not just from the recent future but over the span of my whole life. It was as though the only place my heart felt it could purge itself of these pains was the place I stood, wrapped up as I was. It took some time, but after awhile I stopped crying, the pain left, and I stepped back from Joshua.

I needed that. Even with all the counsel of the universe at his fingertips, he hadn't said anything. Sometimes silence is more healing than words.

We began to walk towards the town, side by side, and it occurred to me that it was the first time I felt fully comfortable to be alone with Joshua. Maybe I was more than comfortable, because the thought of sharing him with someone else now seemed less than ideal.

On our way to Joshua's house, we walked through the village, which had a wood stage constructed in the middle of the town square.

"That stage looks new. Are you having the Embrace's meetings in town rather than the field?" I asked.

"No. Joe Tetzel set that up." Joshua giggled. "He has been preaching on it at nights, trying to get some of the people to 'come to the narrow path that steers away from hell.'"

"Do you think he really believes that you are that dangerous, I mean, that you are willfully deceiving people and leading them to hell?"

"Probably partly."

"It is all so ridiculous. Why are they spending their energy on you, when they could be doing something much more advantageous with their time? It isn't like you have killed anyone or pose any real material threat."

Joshua's head kicked back in amusement and a hooting sound came from his mouth. He had so many different kinds of laughter. "I know! It gives me a good laugh."

We were at the steps to Joshua's house, standing on the front steps. Maybe it was because it weighed so little, being made of silk, but it was only then that I realized that a robe was draped over my shoulders. Joshua must have snuck that in while he was holding me on the road.

"I have to run an errand. I believe Echelon is inside. I will be back shortly."

I bid Joshua goodbye, and walked inside. Echelon was drinking tea at a small table next to large windows that looked out on the garden. He stood to greet me, hugged me, then looked me in the face while holding one hand to my cheek, as if he was inspecting me.

"It was that bad, was it?" He said.

"Yeah, but I will be ok."

"I know you will. Joshua left this for you."

He pointed to the table he had been sitting at. Sitting on a scrap of paper was a large ring, fit with an emerald. I picked up the paper first, reading what was written on it.

Scythe,

I am very proud of you. You will always be apart of my family, and I will never find reason to abandon you. I will always trust you. I will always understand you. Please take this ring as a token of my love and a symbol of my

commitment to you. I will be
faithful to you, forever your friend,
and death will never do us part.
                                    –Joshua

I set down the piece of paper and picked up the ring. It was heavy and bright. On the inside I saw that Joshua had inscribed "Scythe, the honorable king".

I have to say; I didn't fully understand the honor Joshua gave others, including myself. It was without bounds. With the Chosen I had been told that if you honored a man too much it would eventually work to his disadvantage, building up his pride, resulting in his inevitable fall. But Joshua didn't hold back from praising others in the least bit. He was always affirming and honoring those around him, apparently not in the least bit concerned how it would be received.

Yet, from being with Joshua I had learned that it is in the place of extravagant blessing that the heart is most humbled, not in the midst of conviction or being laid bare. The blessing or compliment causes one, if they are willing to be even slightly honest, to come to grip with the fact that they did nothing to earn it. This makes meekness and humility come to life in one's heart in a way that outranks how one feels when their imperfections are highlighted. In fact, helping someone else discover their lackings never leads them to humility. I was learning that it is only by looking at someone through the eyes of Another, in all of their beauty, giftedness, and perfection and then letting them know, that we truly humble them.

It fit perfectly on my finger, and as I slipped it on I noticed something peculiar about the large, translucent, green rock. Inside the emerald was something smoke-like moving about, like it had a will of its own. The rock was solid the whole way through, with no hollow point anywhere inside, nonetheless something seemed to dwell and move within. I watched it closely to see what it would do. Every few minutes it would form itself into a shape, becoming clearer and clearer in detail until the moving picture it was showcasing was unmistakable, then would slowly fade again, taking its time to become like wisp of smoke again. Each picture was a memory of Joshua that I had; one was he jumping off the broken stage in the field, the next was he greeting us the first time I met him.

But the next picture I didn't recognize. I saw Joshua standing over my bed as I slept in my house (the house the Seers assumed was their own and sold). I looked younger and more energetic. Joshua was quietly watching me, wearing the smile that had become so predictable to me.

There was a knock on the door. I answered, and found Joshua back from his errand.

"Do you like the ring?" He asked.

"Yes. It seems wonderfully bewitched."

"Yes. You can't get those stones here. Have you figured out what it reveals?"

"At first I thought it was my memories of the times we were together, but then I saw a picture I don't recall in the least bit."

"Ah, it showed you further back. That is where the real wonder begins. It does not show your memories, but it could be said that it shows mine. Most simply explained, the ring shows anytime we were together, whether you were aware of it or not."

"I'm not sure I follow you. For example, I saw a picture of you standing over me as I slept in my house, but I didn't know you until but a few days ago."

"Yes, but though you have only known me for a few days, I have always known you. You see Scythe, that ring is to heal your heart of all the things that you have witnessed in these last days. What heals a person's heart most from a tragic situation isn't by removing it from their memory, but by recognizing I was there with them in the midst of it. If you watch the ring long enough you will see every circumstance in your life, good or bad, and will learn that I was no further away than an arms length every time. This is the only way to become whole. Every death, rape, and betrayal you ever witnessed was enclosed in and encircled by the reality of my being present, which you didn't know until now, and won't fully know with your heart until you see the pictures. That doesn't make everything right, but better.

I will warn you though. Some of what it will show will be brutal, for what happened at points was brutal. The redemptive thing about that is that the ring will always show more about my being present rather than the brutality of what was happening. This is because my presence is always a greater reality than anything that takes place in this realm. That is, if it is recognized. Hence, the ring.

Also, you may not always remember what you see, for the human mind has a survival mode of forgetfulness for the significant wounds some people have experienced. Anyways, enough warnings. Do you like it?"

"Yes. Thank you. It is a wonderful gift." I said.

"Excellent. Scythe, I have a favor to ask of you."

"Anything, Joshua." I said.

"Well, tonight Joe will be speaking at another one of his rallies in town square. He hasn't been well received here. My people don't fall for intimidating techniques. Not just that, but they are like radars for anything that remotely hints of domination and control. Most of my people have learned the way of peace, but some of those in the Embrace are less seasoned. Remember, we had people just the other night in the field that were new. They can't be expected to know our ways yet, and I am worried that they may, very understandably, react in violence to Joe's words. I want you to go to Joe's crusade tonight and ensure that nothing happens."

I was a bit surprised. "So in essence, you are sending me to be his bodyguard? But Joe is a worm. Do you know the things he has done? Wouldn't it be better to let the consequences of his actions and words take their toll? At least then he would learn."

"No, I am not fond of that. Man doesn't *truly* learn when he learns through fault. That is why men can stumble again and again throughout their life and never change, despite the fact that what they are doing is destroying their relationships with their family and friends. Man only *really* learns when he realizes he has been given kindness when he doesn't deserve it. And yes, I do know the things he has done. Nonetheless, that doesn't permit us to not protect him."

"If anyone else asked me, I would tell them to take a hike. But I will do as you ask, only because it is you asking."

Joshua patted me on the back. "Thank you. Dusk is falling. You may want to get on your way. Joe will be starting soon."

Twenty-Two

I could hear Joe from hundreds of yards away. The scratchy speaker system he was using belted out his intense voice, unmistakeable from far away as I made my way to his crusade. It had been such a long time since I had heard someone yell while they were speaking. It was the kind where there is no pause, just a rambling of words at the highest pitch they can muster until that lungful of air is expelled. Then they gasp and go for another stint.

I wasn't excited to be there.

He was going on about hell, and if we don't do what he said we would inevitably go there because he had been ordained by The Eternal to do such and such a thing. It went on like that for quite a while.

Those that I assume were a part of the Embrace, which was the majority of the crowd, stood around with their arms crossed, frowning at Joe. Joe didn't seem to mind, like the reaction he was aiming for in his hearers was dissatisfaction. And after thinking about it, I realized that was probably exactly what was going on. Joe assumed that if people didn't like what he was saying it was because he was touching on a facet of truth that they had not yet surrendered to, and thus that he was instigating a holy, internal struggle to take place inside of his hearers. In actuality, his message was just plain bad. There was no struggle of truth going on inside us and he was not being used by the Eternal to purify our hearts. We just simply disagreed with him and wished him to shut up.

Then I had a brilliant idea. I reasoned that if he was pleased with our displeasure, then our happiness may have the opposite effect on him. The people would also be in a better mood, which would ensure that they would not attack Joe. It was two birds with one stone.

To bring this shift about, I simply retreated into my spirit. I felt peace and joy come over me, tingling my skin. Before I could stop it (for when you give yourself over like this you never know what unexpected thing you may do), I began to laugh out loud. And it was very loud. Unavoidability loud.

I could have been embarrassed, but embarrassment doesn't really have any grounds to stand on, especially in that town. What was happening to me is immediately infectious if one actually lets it out, and within moments you are not the only one behaving this way. This is exactly what happened. The laughter spread like wildfire throughout the crowd. Soon people were bent at the waist and hunched over, suffering (if you can call it that) from the kind of laughter that you don't have control over. This was the kind of laughter that causes your eyes to tear.

I want to be clear that I wasn't laughing *at* Joe, but definitely, at least in part, because of him. I would look at him and laugh even harder. And he was getting more and more upset. The harder we bellowed, the more intense his preaching got and the redder his face got. It wasn't just that we weren't listening to him anymore, but that he was starting to realize that he didn't have control over even one soul in the crowd. I am sure that was new for him. Poor guy.

His preaching went from the fires of hell and offerings that would save you from punishment, to outright condemnation. He began declaring bad things over the people rather than just talking about them happening if we lived in disobedience. But the sound of joy was drowning him out, not in disrespect, but just because nobody was paying any attention to him anymore. The screeching of the sound system he had been yelling into showed me that its volume was already maxed out and couldn't be turned up anymore. He tried to shout over the crowd's noise, but it was a losing battle. He finally threw down the microphone and walked off the stage.

I wasn't sure if there was someone in the crowd who had taken Joe's words personally and thus may want retaliation, so I figured that I had better follow Joe to ensure his safety. He walked behind the stage and was met by a young woman that helped him slip his coat on. I assumed the woman was his assistant. But who knew, knowing Joe. Though he was a religious man, Joe indulged in anything he wanted to, and the rumors said that at times it was young girls. That was just the start. It was said that he didn't just find company with young women, though he was married, but that he wasn't slow to do unspeakable things to the daughters of men he was questioning for treason. I won't go into details, but I will say that if there was one person I can say that I hated, it was Joe Tetzel. I didn't just hate him for his hypocrisy, but because the evils he bathed in were not the common transgressions that most men may wade in and out of throughout their life. The things he did were indescribably wicked, perverse, and detestable.

They walked down a long, dark alley. I stayed a safe distance behind them, watching for anyone that may come up behind him and clunk him over the head with a steel pipe or two-by-four. It isn't just the righteous that people want to assassinate, but also scum like Joe that have no more value than the residue one scrapes off the bottom of their shoe before they enter their house. In this life, both the righteous and unrighteous are hunted, thus I stayed close enough to intercept anyone trying to make a move on his life, but far enough away that I wouldn't be noticed.

I could hear Joe talking, making out what he was saying here and there. He was still angry on account of his tone, and his brisk step communicated that he was eager to get back to his room.

I got a bit closer, and his voice became more clear at the precise moment that he started talking about shaking the dust off his feet and moving on to a more receptive town. The offerings had been far less than what he had anticipated. Then he said, "That means that before we leave, we must execute the last portion of our mission. We have no other choice! Have you burned enough treated wood?"

The woman next to him, acting more like a servant than assistant, reverently said, "Yes, my Lord."

"And have you concentrated the remains so that the arsenic is strong enough for him?"

"Yes, without a doubt, my Lord."

"Very good. Now come in and help me ready for bed."

They had reached a doorstep, opened it, and entered. Joe was safe, and I was free to go back to Joshua's house.

As I walked along the road and through the dark, Joe's words echoed in my head over and over. I knew what

Joe was planning on doing. He wanted to poison someone, and I believed I knew who.

Joshua was standing in the garden waiting for me to return. "Everything go peacefully?" He asked.

"Yes. But I need to talk to you about something."

"Okay. Shoot."

"I followed Joe back to his room after he had spoken at the rally. Something I overheard him say has stuck with me, and gives me the most awful feeling. He was talking about the last part of his mission, and something about arsenic. I can only deduce that he intends to poison someone, and I would guess that someone is you."

"Ah, delightful!"

"What? How is that delightful?"

"I received an invitation from Joe to dinner tomorrow night. He said I could bring a guest. Would you like to come?"

"Joshua, did you hear what I said? He intends to poison you at the dinner!"

"It wouldn't surprise me. But will you come? I would love to spend the time with you."

"Yes, I will come. Tell me that you heard what I said, if not just for me."

"I did. Now let us get some rest."

184 | THE COMING

Twenty-Three

*T*he next day went quickly, and I soon found myself a few hours from dinner. Joshua loaned me some of his clothes, as he told me that Joe likely thought this meal was to be a formal one. We dressed, bid Echelon goodbye, and went on our way.

Joe answered the door to the little house he was renting while in town, and looked quite joyful that we were there. I was altogether aware as to why.

Conversation was the shallow type; talking of things that matter very little and cause no real connection to come about between people. Joe probably liked it that way. Though he was being hospitable, he was nonetheless distant and closed off.

We sat down before a meager meal that Joe's assistant had scrounged up. The most impressive part of the meal was three large wine glasses, filled to the brim with well-aged Pinot Noir. Joe said some formal prayer of thanksgiving, through which Joshua kept his eyes opened, hands unfolded like Joes, smiling and looking right at our host. As soon as Joe ended the prayer and bid us drink, Joshua spoke.

"Joe, I know what you have done to this drink, as does Scythe. I wanted you to know that I know."

And before Joe could defend himself in claiming ignorance to what Joshua was saying, Joshua picked up the glass, put it to his lips, and drank every drop in one large guzzling.

I was completely taken back. Before I blurted anything out I caught myself, remembering that Joshua always had some kind of ace up his sleeve that nobody else knew about. He may not have always been in *control* per say, but he always looked like it afterwards because there wasn't any time he didn't come out on top. He took everything thrown at himself and those he loved and transformed it into something that one could stand back and admire.

I hadn't drank alcohol since I was with the Chosen, though I had prior to my membership in excess. Over my time in the Chosen I had gotten my excessiveness under control through simply abstaining from it completely. I was glad for this. But in the meantime I had also made some judgments about alcohol that, if I am honest, had made me look down upon *anyone* that partook, even if they didn't have a problem like I had. I just lumped everyone together, thinking they were as problematic as I had been. Now that Joshua had downed his glass, I had to reevaluate things once again, and saw the pride of my stance. He seemed to have that effect on me quite a lot.

I figured that if Joshua drank it must not be as bad as I had once assumed. Holiness was one thing he did not lack.

So, as a demonstration of my confidence in him on various levels, I did the same as Joshua had. I looked right at Joe thus letting him know I knew my wine was poisoned as well, tossed back the drink like it was water, and set the empty glass down on the table while staring right at Joe unwaveringly.

Joe was speechless. Joshua smiled, and I felt a camaraderie well up between us. After a few moments, as if he hadn't heard Joshua or seen what we had done, he picked up the shallow conversation we had been having, never acknowledging what we had just done.

Joshua hadn't touched his food but suddenly stood and thanked Joe for his time.

"You are already leaving? But we haven't eaten yet!" Joe said.

"I am aware of that. But there is no reason to not be honest about the fact that your whole intended purpose for tonight was just fulfilled. There is now no reason for us to stay. Wouldn't you agree?"

Joe was trying to hold his own, but his face was wearing the same confusion that Joshua had caused me when I first met him. Joshua had a way of running circles around someone that thought they were they were in charge. The confounded look on Joe's face was swept away by the veneer of cheerfulness, and he then stood to say goodnight.

"I suppose it is getting late. Have a wonderful walk back, my friends. It was quite nice to meet you both! Sleep well!" Joe said as we walked out and he closed the door behind us.

"I hope you know what you are doing." I said mumbled under my breath as we walked away.

"It is all in good fun." Joshua cackled.

"Is that the wine talking? You *do* know what you are doing, right?"

Joshua's face went blank and he looked at me without smile or smirk. "Scythe. Everything will be fine."

It was then that I realized that he was only serious when I needed him to be. The rest of the time he was so lighthearted and carefree that he reminded me of what I imagined a stranger would be like, seated next to you, that simply laughs when they are given the information that the roller-coaster you are riding has just detached from the tracks. He was, in every sense, disconcerting to logic and reason, yet never made you uncomfortable in a way that made peace leave your side. Like I said, I had learned that he always had a plan, even if it was hidden away in a place that I couldn't see. This, I suspected, is what made him so unworried in very troubling circumstances. The result to the fact that he had a plan was that I was safe, regardless of what was happening, would happen, or in this case, had just happened.

"Ok. I believe you when you say that." The cobblestones of the path that wove through the garden were now underfoot, and our pace slowed as we both looked side to side to see the flowers in the moonlight. "Tell me this; how can the Seers, or Joe for that matter, legitimize in their own hearts their desire to be rid of you, even if that means to engage in murder? How can they justify murder when killing another person was so clearly outlined in scripture as something we are not to do under any circumstances?"

Joshua chuckled. "I guess that depends upon what verses you are accentuating. Just as scripture can be used to affirm the fact that human's should not take life, it can be used just as easily to justify taking a life, especially when one feels that the outcome and result of doing so will seem to work towards mankind's good or the 'will of god'. Bonhoeffer came to this crossroad. Thus, people weigh situations on an unseen balancing scale in their heart, trying to feel out if the end justifies the means. Many times they come to the conclusion that it does.

The Seers have convinced themselves that I am of the utmost threat to what the Eternal has commissioned them to do, which is to lead and shepherd the people. After one has tired themselves with talk and logic they very quickly (and especially when you believe that god is on your side and your side only) come to a place of believing that the only sure solution to the problem is to erase the source of the problem. Much has been done in the name of protecting the truth or carrying out the will of The Eternal. And so here we are."

"Is it really that simple?"

"Probably not. It is probably much more complicated than that; complicated in philosophical ways that we are better off not trying to understand. But as far as how they legitimize murder in their hearts, there are many ways. This type of thing isn't the first time this has happened. I've been through this exact thing before, don't forget. Their logic is still the same, leaping to assumptions that lead to drastic measures on their behalf.

And since then, the crusades, the various inquisitions, the bombing of abortion clinics, and the wars fought over religious purposes all point to the fact that men still believe that The Eternal *may*, at points, will them to take life. Even in scripture, some men seemed to have been given a weekend pass to walk outside the boundary lines of one of the Ten Commandments; Thou shall not kill. It is all very curious.

But I am telling you now; to take a life is not needed. The Eternal does not, did not, and will not ever, will for anyone to die. There are more redemptive and creative ways to deal with situations that seem to be immovable."

"I agree. I remember believing that taking a life would help our mission move forward when I was in the Unenlightened, but it always backfired. We would kill off one of the Chosen and ten more would rise up in their place. It would have been much more effective to simply ignore them than make them our rivals."

"True." Joshua said. We were now near the house. "And I believe that there is one more thing that is at work in the Seers that causes them to believe that what they are doing is right.

It is this; men become who they believe their god is. This is true even if they have got it wrong and He is nothing like what they think. If one believes that The Eternal is angry, sooner or later they will become like their god and exert anger. It may be a slow process, but it is nonetheless always taking shape within. If one believes that The Eternal doesn't have grace for people in the midst of sin, they most likely will think and talk of punishment and wrath and sooner or later find that they are unwilling to extend grace to those around them when a situation arises where grace is needed. One becomes what they behold. And in this case, if one believes that there is any point in which the Eternal will take life, then they will find themselves arriving at that same point. Sometimes it sneaks up on them without their knowledge of it, then one day it is heaved up in an instant. The person stands there amazed, looking at what they just brought out of depths of themselves, splattered all over a fellow man. It may not always look like overt murder in the outright sense, but they take life nonetheless; murdering the dreams, relationships, confidence, and ministries of others.

When one possess such beliefs, the heart living within that gives real convictions, convictions born into every human and the sort that make you sick when you push against them, slowly dries up and dies. Then inevitably, they will run across circumstances in which their religious belief outweighs the convictions laid away in their dying heart, and thus, will be able to legitimize the actions they want to take.

They came to this conclusion, without any doubt, because at some point they believed that The Eternal will take life if the cause is great enough."

"I was there once. The Eternal help them." I said.

"Yes. Well that is enough of that. Just talking about it feels heavy. We have more impending things pressing upon us. Tomorrow is a very important day."

"It is?"

"Yes. Tomorrow is the Day of Levitation."

"I have never heard of such a day." I said, as I climbed the steps to Joshua's house.

"Yes you have. It is not merely a gathering, but the gathering. Tomorrow you will understand. Sleep deep, and without fear of what swims in your blood from Joe's little stunt. I will see you tomorrow."

Twenty-Four

The Embrace must have gotten the word out about the next day being one of special importance, for when I awoke and went into town I found the whole place moving, everyone hustling and bustling about. People weren't really doing anything of any real importance like buying food for lunch or running their shops, but instead they were just talking and walking here and there. Some even just walked back and forth in a straight line like one would do if they were extremely anxious. I watched long enough to see that they weren't anxious, just plain excited. There was an unmistakable buzz in the air and just watching the people made it well up in me as well. Something was about to happen.

Just as I was about to ask a few people standing nearby what the excitement was all about, Joshua came walking down the road that led through town with a crowd that I couldn't see the end of following behind him. Those that I had been watching meander about streamed to him, the crowd enclosing all around him. I fought my way through his fans, or lovers as he would call them, and grabbed his hand.

"Scythe! Wonderful to see you! Try to stay next to me."

I held his hand tight, but if you have ever played in the waves at a beach where there is a considerable rip tide you would know what it felt like trying to walk beside Joshua in that crowd. One wave of people would pummel me from my right, and then the entire crowd would push in another direction, sucking me away from him, constantly keeping me off balance. I held to his hand firmly, at points wondering if it was hurting him because I gripped him so intensely in order that I didn't lose him. At first I was worried by the playful battering that was a result of Joshua's enthusiasts trying to get near him, that is, until I saw Joshua completely enjoying it. After that I became more fluid and relaxed, allowing myself to go wherever the crowd went, except still holding to Joshua's hand. I couldn't see much of anything but the mass of bodies and dust in the air, everything moving. Once in a while I would see more than just the hand and arm of Joshua. He was laughing and enjoying every moment.

It occurred to me that it wasn't just that his followers adored him, but that they were desperate for him. It wasn't a desperation that came from an unmet need but one that flowed from a growing obsession. Even in the midst of all the flying dirt and sweaty bodies, it was lovely. True love is rarely neat, clean, and concise.

The dust slowly dissipated, though the crowd kept its movement. I looked at the ground and saw coats and leafy plants paving our way, cutting down on the flying debris, the crowd now almost out of town. It looked as though we were headed towards the field where I had seen Joshua paint the sky and move the stars.

"Joshua!" I shouted. "Are we headed to the field?"

"Yes!"

The feeling that something was about to happen hadn't left me yet, and as we triumphantly exited the town I wondered what significant thing lay but a few hundred yards away that would give me such a feeling of anticipation.

Grass was underfoot when we stopped. Joshua was hoisted upon the shoulders of two large men, from where he began to speak.

"It is time to gather those that are mine!" The crowd cheered deafeningly. After a few minutes they quieted again, waiting for what he had to say.

"The earth is about to be ushered into a great period of life. The same way that life flourishes in a wood after it has been destroyed by a forest fire, so will the earth experience abundance. Beauty sprouts from the richness in ash. Everything will be made new. In the meantime, we will go to a place where fire cannot destroy, a place that is already new yet more ancient than any where else."

I think I understood what Joshua was saying, but it confused me.

"But Joshua," I said loudly, the crowd nearby turning and looking at me. "why must we leave? I am not opposed to leaving, but I find little need for it. You have taught me that Heaven is not mostly a place, but a Person. Where you are is where heaven is."

To my surprise, the crowd agreed with me. They cheered.

He laughed and said, "Scythe, have I told you lately that I really like you?" He looked back and forth over the crowd. "It is a very good point, is it not?" Numerous people nodded, then he continued.

"Many here are wondering the same thing. We leave not because we have been defeated, or even because there is more to have there than what anyone can have here if only they believe.

But one does not want to be married in an office building or drab place of that sort, but a mansion or a field of flowers. What comes next can only happen in a place where beauty spans so far and wide that no eye has ever beheld all of it. And there," He began to cry, "we will become as we should have been all along."

Joshua cupped his hands to his mouth, took a large breath, and what came from his mouth was unlike anything I have ever heard before in my life. The sound was strong like steel, moving quickly and sweeping over us, feeling as though it was bending any material thing that got in its way. The sound wave (for I do not know what else to call it) shook my insides and entailed a sentence:

"Come unto me, all you who are weary and burdened, and I will give you rest."

He said it four times, in four directions, and then paused. I wondered if he would say it a fifth time by the way he was sitting forward, but he didn't. Everyone fell silent, waiting for what was to happen next. Something magnetic had just been released. It felt like Joshua had suddenly made the place we were standing the center of the universe and at any moment everything in the earth would be uprooted and come fall upon us, or fold into us like matter does with a black hole.

I doubt that anyone there was ready for what followed. Quite unexpectedly, in the midst of such a sanctified moment, the sound of cursing broke into the air. I don't mean cursing in the sense of what a witch may do to her enemy, but the kind of curse words that may come out of one's mouth when they stub their toe. On second thought, it was possibly a mix of both. This was a torrent of words strung together by expletives. Everyone in the crowd spun around, looking for the person that was so upset in such a reverent moment. I noticed that the voice was getting louder, and that the crowd was parting on one side of me to let someone through.

It was Joe. He looked awful, In fact, awful would have been a compliment. He looked downright haggard and deathly, and was making a line towards Joshua, it now clear that he wasn't merely swearing to swear, but swearing at him.

"Joe!" Joshua thundered. "Come to me at once!" I was surprised to hear him raise his voice.

"I won't do it! You need to listen to me for once!" Joe hollered back. "I have had enough of you. If you don't serve a god that is angry, then why did this happen to me? Is this their judgment and justice?" (I am of course leaving out the vulgarities that were scattered amidst his sentences.)

"Joe, come to me at once before it is too late!" Joshua yelled. I knew he wasn't the least bit angry, only because I knew he wasn't like that, but to anyone that didn't know him I am sure they would have mistaken the urgency in his voice for rage.

"I said I won't do it! You can't control me and tell me to do this or that and think that I will just do as you say, heretic!"

Joe was still moving towards Joshua, and the closer he got to me, the more I saw of Joe's state. His fingernails were discolored and what looked like vomit had stained his shirt. Every few steps he would convulse in the most disturbing way, showing that he was only in partial control of his body. He carried a knife in his right hand, gripping it tightly.

"You will pay, you devil. No more will your deception blind these poor souls, for..."

His voice trailed off. He stopped walking forward, stood still, and a surprised look swept over his face. Then he simply collapsed, wilting to the ground. He lay there motionless. Nobody in the crowd jumped forward to help him. His pathetic frame was outstretched on the grass. Someone calmly bent down and took the knife out of his hand as Joshua got down from the shoulders of the two men and made his way over to him.

"Silly boy", Joshua said as he stood over Joe's body. He bent down and cradled Joe's head and upper body in his lap, and whispered something under his breath. Immediately Joe's eyes opened, as though Joshua had just awakened him from a light nap. It seemed that all of Joe's energy and life had been restored for he quickly lurched back, out of Joshua's lap and away from him.

"What did you do to me, devil? Why were you touching me?"

"Joe, I will not harm you. Look at your fingers. The poison is gone." The pigmentation had left his fingernails, and the convulsions had ceased.

"So you made me well. Just another one of your tricks. I am sure I will be sick again as soon as I leave. Probably imparted demons to me while you were at it too, eh! Never touch me again. Do you not know the Holy Scriptures? 'Touch not the Lord's anointed!' I am surprised that you can lead so many people when you are so daft. Any twit knows that verse. You obviously lack knowledge, thus respect, of the Holy Scriptures!"

He kept rambling on and on like this. For some reason, it was embarrassing for anyone to watch though Joe was the one that should have been embarrassed. It felt the same way as when one witnesses someone else's pants accidently fall down in public. *They* are the ones that lost their pants, but oddly, *you* find yourself embarrassed. So it was here.

"I am not sure how I got sick in the first place." Joe glared at Joshua. "How did the arsenic get into my cup unless you put it there? You must have switched the glasses. Trying to take my life, eh? I thought you were not one for that, hypocrite!"

"I did not switch the glasses. Joe, we are about to go to the lands of ecstasy, in the countries of matrimony. Would you like to come with us? I would deeply value your company there." Joshua said calmly, with such authenticity that it, I have to admit, slightly offended me. I wasn't exactly *excited* to have Joe tag along.

"What? Preposterous! Answer me, devil, why you made me sick in the first place! I command thee!" Joe coughed out.

"I didn't. You made yourself sick."

"You are ridiculous! That is what was supposed to happen to you!"

"Exactly. One cannot engage in such an act and darkness not use their choice as an open door to afflict them. I desire that people not engage in sin because it will harm them, not because I get mad when they do. This is the one of the first things you need to learn about me. But perhaps before that you need to know the plain truth; I did not poison you."

"Shut up. I will not hear another word. You will not infect me with your teachings."

"Maybe not, but I do not need to. I already stole your heart the moment I drank of the wine in your house, didn't I?"

"Never."

"You are lying, Joe." Joshua's voice was gentler than I had ever heard it before. He spoke so quietly you could barely hear it, like he didn't want others to hear. I knew Joshua well enough to guess that this was because he didn't want Joe to be dishonored by his honesty. "You respected the courage of it, the lack of fear. It gave you a rush to see someone so unflinching in the face of death."

"*You* are the liar, Sir." Joe, still sitting on the grass, spit on the ground next to Joshua. Joshua made no note of Joe's action, and continued as tranquil as ever.

"Joe, there is nothing I can say or do to convince you. I know that. But please, remember what I am about to tell you. I know every single thing you ever did. Much of it was rotten. But I also see the good. I see what you have done in secret, not just the bad, but the good things that you have done and hidden away so that your reputation wasn't blunted down. And after I have seen everything you are and have done, this is my conclusion; I love you. I want you to be with me."

Joe paused. I thought that for a second Joshua got through to him, because he sat there taking in what Joshua had just said. Then like the suddenness of the explosion from a bomb, Joe responded with the most pathetic and ear-shattering scream.

"I DO NOT WANT YOUR LOVE. I WANT YOUR REPENTANCE!"

The outburst didn't seem to deter Joshua, nor cause him to jump back like many did in the crowd when it surprised them. Once again, he calmly responded.

"I know what you want. It is peace. Joe, I am telling you, we are about to leave. The place we are going is the most peaceful, beautiful place ever made, but I am the only door you will find to enter through. There is no other way. Come with us, my friend."

"I am *not* your friend. And peace and beauty matter not to me if they are not true. The place you refer to is darkness, and you will probably have these people drink kool-aid to get there, right? If you really are going somewhere, and somehow taking all these people with you, especially without trucks or trains," he laughed mockingly, "then go! I would like to see it!"

"Farewell Joe. You are welcome to come to me anytime you decide to. Remember what I said."

And with that, Joshua stood from the ground and walked away from Joe, back to the center of the group. The hole that had opened up around Joe closed again, and everyone's attention was directed back to Joshua.

"Many are waiting for us. It is time."

And with that Joshua raised his hands slowly. As he did, I felt my insides rise, like how falling makes one feel when taking a sudden dip on a ride at a theme park, only the other way around. I began to feel light, not in head, but physically. Every part of me felt as though for my whole life it had been weighed down and that now those weights were being lifted off me. My arms wanted to float by my side rather than hang from my shoulders. My legs didn't feel like they were carrying the rest of me anymore, but just suspended below me, though I was standing quite normally on the ground. Maybe it was that the center of my being and balance was changing, or maybe it was something different altogether, but I had never felt this way before. I couldn't tell which way was up or down, as though it didn't matter anymore. Then for a split second I thought that I wasn't on the ground at all anymore. I reasoned that was impossible, looked down (*if* it was down, for everything was jumbled together now), and saw that I was firmly planted on the ground. But then it happened again, and this time I noticed others there too. It wasn't that we were necessarily floating, but just going somewhere else.

I saw Joshua there with us, escorting the way. He was pulling others from different places, even deep corners, the way a magnet picks up bits of metal as it is drug along the ground. He was not particular in who he took (at least not in the way the Seers would have been), especially drawing the poor and uneducated, exemplifying his lack of exclusiveness. It seemed to me that he felt that anyone would do, but it became clear that though some may have not known his name, they *did* all have a peculiar sort of recognition in their eyes when they locked gaze with him. Some were reverently silent as they arrived, the way a servant would act before a king that they knew about but didn't know quite how to address him. I assumed that they were quiet because they questioned if the names they had used for him were now fitting enough to address him as such. Some of them even had a bit of surprise on their face, like they had finally found the thing they had looked for after a long time. Others seemed to be very well acquainted with him. Thus our crowd grew and grew. I was only able to take in parts of everything that was happening because it felt like my mind was over going a significant change, like the reformatting an electrical device goes through when a new update becomes available. What I was experiencing both confused and clarified things at the same time.

And though Joshua seemed quite busy with what he was doing, he turned back to look at me and said, "We are almost there... But there is a question you have for me, no?"

"Yes. It feels wrong to bring it up now, what with everyone gathering to us like they are. But I must confess that I am not excited about Joe ever joining us. Though, now that I think of it, I do also feel some sadness for him that he didn't come with us."

"Part of you doesn't want him with us because you think that will mean that you will have to share me with him. Rest assured; you will never have to share me again, not in the way you know. Sharing there doesn't mean something is partitioned up so that everyone gets less, but more. You will have as much of me as you desire.

Another part of you doesn't want him with us because you assume that he will be the same burden that he was before. That won't be the case. In fact, there are few people I like to be with as much as Joe when he is in enough liberty to be himself. Many think that it is the original design of a person that is irreversibly flawed, thinking it needs to die off altogether and replaced with something new. But in actuality, when my love invades a person's heart, I simply make them more *them*. When Joe is being fully *Joe*, he is an absolute hoot to be with.

And considering the interactions you had with Joe, the fact that you feel any sadness for him at all points to the fact that a distinct measure of maturity has come into your possession. Love is becoming more than a choice for you, something of instinct, the miraculous sort. Don't fret; Joe will fold. It will just take time. Redemption is for all, but it is every person's choice to reach out and receive it. My goal isn't to force redemption to happen, but to make it available to the worst of us. That may take more time, but I am not anxious about it, like many assume. It takes time, but I do it like this because when it does happen, everyone has come willingly and on their own accord rather than simply because I want it. I won't override what Joe wants, though I will do my best to influence it. I respect him too much to do anything more, or less.

Yes, do not fret my friend. My words of love will haunt him until what drives him in such religious devotion will finally relent. He will be exhausted from the chase and will have no more energy to go on trying to shield his heart from my love. One day he will surrender. And I know that right now it may not sound like much fun to you to have him there with us, but you never got to see Joe with his walls lowered. He is a wonderful person when he isn't trying to be religious. As it is with any of us!"

I chuckled and he winked in return, for Joshua had seen me at a few of my most religiously zealous moments.

Then suddenly, everyone but Joshua was gone and we were alone. Unseen hands seemed to be undressing him, and my first reaction was to turn away from him in order to give him his privacy, but before I had the chance to turn it occurred to me that he wasn't being undressed at all but was being revealed as he really was. If anything, he was being clothed with what was his all along. What came from him cannot be described as bright, for even the brightest of the sun's light can't compare to the whiteness of the radiance that came from him. It was not light in the way that we understand it, but living waves of life that poured from him, filling every space around me. It moved right through my body and shot out the other side, as though my body had the same material density to it as air. Flesh and blood caused it no resistance, and though some sifted through me, some also stayed behind, inside me. I watched it swirl and jet about like weightless liquid, defying gravity. It was so beautiful and intriguing that I forgot for a moment who was its source.

"This is my normal attire. Do you like it?" He said, breaking me from my thoughts. I had mentally drifted off somehow, mesmerized by the movement around us. Much time had passed, though I don't know how much, and I realized that merely the glory that rested upon him was enough to captivate me for tens, maybe even hundreds, of years.

"You are glorious, my friend." I said.

Joshua looked away as if to peer into the distance, then turned back to me and said. "We are there. The food is warm, the table is set, and the wine has been poured. Come enjoy the fullness of my embrace."

As we moved forward He reached over and wiped away tears I did not know I was crying. Then I was awash in light, its liquid all around me, and the only thing I was conscious of was that I was with One that I loved.

Epilogue

Well, that is my account. I can say that what most people looked forward to before coming here, which was for the pain and tears to cease, is now but a past, fading memory. The nearness we experience was a far more authentic reality. One feels as though they can faint from delight at every moment. It is a consistent, sustained thing.

We did go back. And many stayed. Many more lived in both places. I have chosen to stay here, at least most of the time. Every once and awhile I go down, but I enjoy the burning light of this place much more. It hurt at first, but my eyes and skin became used to it. Now it feels as though I even need its nearly incinerating whiteness. But that is my preference.

And as for below, it looks very different. Many prefer it there, mainly for its greenness. Everything grows with much life, order, and age.

When I say order, I don't mean in the boorish lines that man would call "order" when planting his gardens. The unpredictable wildness of placement that plants and trees grew by when we were there before is still the same, but the kind of parasitical behavior that nature had before it was made new is now removed. No tree grows out of another that had died. Vines don't swallow trees. The result is an undefined order in that everything respects the life of everything else. Nothing needs to feed on anything else because there is enough life in the air and soil to do without that lecherous behavior.

The absence of death changed everything, but some

of the smallest changes are often times what gathers my attention most. For example, there were no fermenting leaves about the ground. Fruit, if not eaten, does not rot on the ground but immediately becomes another plant or tree. In fact, you could still eat the apple that an old apple tree grew from, if you could find it in the mass of all of the roots, deep below. Everything is completely preserved, if that is a fitting word at all. It isn't because there is nothing to preserve from.

An obvious note is that there are plants and trees there that we had never seen in our previous life, but what stole my curiosity was the stages in the growth of growing things. Plants don't just grow, they become something new altogether because their growth is so unlimited and unhindered now. If there was something you liked before, say a rose, it will not be gone, only added to if you watch it long enough. That leaves us with the beauty of what we had before, plus much more.

For example, the orchid I saw with Joshua must have only been in its second stage, for I saw an orchid there that I assumed was one step past that. It beheld a flower, but the flower had sprouted another flower out of itself, so that it was flower upon flower, without need of stem, root, or dirt. Not far from where I saw this layering of flowers, I saw what I can barely call an orchid. I suppose it was in its fourth stage, for it had grown as large as a tree. The yellow and white flowers (though they were never limited to these colors) were countless, and the air for miles around was thick with its aroma. It looked like a twenty foot tall woman giant that had grown out her dense, curly blonde hair long enough to touch the ground. And when the wind blew it was if she was slightly rolling her head back in order to clear the hair that covered her face, the way a woman does while dancing to attract a man. The flowers would part and any bystander would see inside where the stem was, now trunk, and what it nursed within; the purple berry had grown to the size of a melon. I assumed it was capable of taking the hunger of a small nation away for a few days. Many times I withdrew from my desire to consume the entire thing, thinking it selfish and gluttonous of myself, but one day I folded and picked it. It was not hard to devour every last bit. It filled me at the first touch to my tongue, but the taste caused me to continue eating. Normally this would have resulted in being over-full, with the discomfort that we have all felt when walking away from a buffet, but I was pleased to discover that no matter how much I ate, I never became too full. It was just right, though I kept eating. And soon I found that it was not selfish of me to indulge in this berry-melon alone, for I forgot that just as the berry had in Joshua's garden, it would grow right back, as it did before my eyes.

Because I had found the further stages of growth for the orchid, I went to find the same for a pine tree. I knew to look for its telltale sky-blue flowers, and I soon found a row of pines that were all at different places in their growth. One was as I remembered it; clothed in blue. The next must have been a bit further in years, for its branches were longer, hanging down instead of reaching out, forming a rounder shape when I stood back to look at it. It looked like a monstrous weeping willow that had sprouted indigo blooms, for they had darkened in color. It reminded me of a mother reaching down to shelter her children, so I walked up to its huge base and stepped through the wall of flowers that the arms presented. I was surprised to find a wonderful area inside, like a circular room with a large pillar in the middle.

If one wanted to be alone, this was the place to set out for. Another pine nearby was halfway through a stage, or so I presumed. It looked as though it was becoming two trees, splitting itself right down the middle. I found out later that they literally divide, the way cells do, then walk away from each other. Abundant life is like that; even roots can become like feet. What was stationary before can now dance, what was silent can now sing.

We quickly moved from the previous black and white way of thinking that we had all held of our surroundings, in terms of editable or uneatable, to a more broad understanding of nutriment and fare. This isn't just because what would have once harmed us is now curbed in its intensity and defensiveness, but because our bodies now make use of parts of itself that it never used before. The function of whole organs, despite our scientific advances in those days, were unknown prior to this Remaking. Only now do we witness their intended use. Everything can be eaten and delighted in without drawback or harm. The problem of hunger is a memory nearly forgotten by us all. Foxglove, lilies, oleanders, and plums were all set on the same plain. Many times He would fill whole tables, spilling off every side, with these redeemed delicacies, overflowing with beauty and overwhelming to the eye, then bid us sit and eat. What we could only enjoy with sight and smell before was now able to give itself to the sons of men wholly. You have never tasted such elation.

On my visits, I noticed that dwelling places didn't serve the same purpose as they had before. They were built only for the purpose of extravagance, never shelter, for the elements are not as they had been before. Weather never works against man like it had earlier, but serves him. Thus, man has no need to protect himself from the earth like he had. It is just as pleasurable, peaceful, and comfortable to bed down in a patch of grass as it was to stay in a place comparable to Buckingham Palace, if not better in the grass. Structures and abodes are now constructed for the reasons of beauty, accomplishment, and art. Many did so to provide a place for Him on His travels to the lower regions, but we all knew that He would be just as delighted to lay His head in the dust if it was to lay it besides one of ours. He is just like that.

Thus, man can live anywhere, and when I say that I mean it in the most literal sense. I first discovered this when I was following a friend I had been reunited with. He had something to show me, and told me to follow close behind him as he led the way to it. When we were not far from a large lake, he began to sprint, tell me to keep up with him. He got to the edge of the water in a spot where the water lapped up against a small cliff, and dove. I followed him in, but when I came to the surface he wasn't there. I had supposed we were going to swim across the lake, with what he wanted to show me on the other side of it. Looking down and opening my eyes, I could make out as clear as if I had a scuba mask on that he was still swimming down, headed for the bottom of the lake. He turned, waved me to him, and knowing that there was no harm that could befall me in this place, I followed.

You know the sort of dream where you find yourself underwater and in a traumatic state of mind because the surface is far above you, making a dash for its air nearly impossible? You try and fail, then do what one never wants to do and you open your mouth from instinct to inhale. That breath comes in thick, like you would expect, but surprisingly, somehow satisfies your need for air. The tension leaves, and you start to enjoy yourself there under the water. That was much like what happened when I followed my friend to the bottom of that lake. When I say that man can inhabit anywhere there because the elements are for him rather than against him, that is what I mean. The whole earth is his again.

As for "travel", what we did was very different from what you know of. We have no need for cars and planes, for our thoughts served us the same way those large, metal contraptions of man did, yet our travel is much quicker, and safety is never an issue.

The food is inexplicably grand. We eat because we can, not because we have to. What we called the best of a king's supper is nothing more than cardboard compared to what we eat there. The obvious point is that taste and texture was magnified, but what is more curious is how the food itself affects us. Everything we eat is alive, somehow giving itself to us, not to die, but to live in us forever, forever making us stronger. Food, like the weather, serves us in the most extraordinary ways. What we consume *wants* to be eaten by us, Kings as we are. As Hwin said to the Lion, "You are so beautiful. I would rather be eaten by you than fed by anyone else", so it is true with us. What we eat does not die within us but is assimilated into our bodies, with nothing leftover, not digested as we used to do. There is nothing leftover because there is no need to be rid of anything. Everything is life. Everything is alive.

All speak the same language, one that you, reader, have never heard. Its beauty doesn't compare to any tongue on earth, and the best I can describe it to you is to say that it is more sung than spoken, the way whales do. And though we can, we rarely use our mouth to perform it. Our thoughts communicate much more clearly and quickly than our lips ever could, plus distance presents no challenge to us now. This way spans distances we could never reach, and much more instantly. In a moment we can download what it would take someone years to communicate.

And if you spoke it, dear reader, all the words in this volume would have only taken you but a moment to understand. If you spoke our language, you and I would know each other intimately, instantly, as we will soon.

If you would like to continue
this journey with Joshua,
The UnRedeemed is the
sequel to the book
you just read.

OneGlance.org

Made in the USA
Charleston, SC
11 October 2012